# Sist

I spotted a small sheet of paper with Pippa's handwriting on it.

*I know you're not interested, but I'm going to tell you my idea anyway. I think you should ask Amanda to impersonate you for the afternoon when Craig comes over. Craig won't realize she's not you, and everything will be just fine.*

I stared at Pippa's note.
Amanda? *Impersonate* me?
Well done, Pippa – that was your craziest idea yet.
On the other hand, maybe it was just stupid enough to work!

# LITTLE SISTER

## 6

# Sister Switch

**Allan Frewin Jones**

**Series created by Ben M. Baglio**

**RED FOX**

Dedication: *For Kath, Paul, Conor and Sydney*

A Red Fox Book

Published by Random House Children's Books
20 Vauxhall Bridge Road, London SW1V 2SA

A division of Random House UK Ltd
London Melbourne Sydney Auckland
Johannesburg and agencies throughout the world

1 3 5 7 9 10 8 6 4 2

First published in Great Britain by Red Fox 1995

Phototypeset in 12/14 Plantin Roman by Intype, London

Printed and bound in Great Britain by
Cox & Wyman, Reading, Berkshire

RANDOM HOUSE UK Limited Reg. No. 954009

ISBN 0 09 938431 0

# Chapter One

RRRRRRRIIIIINNNNNNGGGGGGGGG!

Have you ever seen an entire class jump two feet into the air? Until that alarm clock went off it had been totally quiet in our classroom. The only sound you could hear was the scratching of pens on paper and the occasional groan as someone got to a question straight out of their nightmares.

'What on earth is going on?' Ms Fenwick bounded up out of her seat as though it had suddenly bitten her.

'Ow! Owowowowow!' Betsy Jane Garside was sitting right in front of me and she started howling in pain because she'd jabbed her pencil in her eye when the alarm clock had gone off.

We were in the middle of a maths test. I was on Question Twelve. These two guys were travelling towards each other on trains. One of them had left Town A at six o'clock in the morning and was travelling east at eighty five miles an hour. The other guy had left town B at eight o'clock and was going west at seventy miles an hour. The towns were five hundred miles apart and we were supposed to figure out where and when the two guys would meet. If you ask me, they could have saved everyone a whole lot of trouble if they'd just *called* each other on the phone.

I was sitting there with my pencil in my mouth, gazing out of the window and imagining these two trains charging towards each other. But the question didn't mention whether they were on the same track. If they *were* on the same track, then I was thinking that the question should really read: *Where and at what time will the two trains crash into each other?*

I guess you're not supposed to wonder about stuff like that in the middle of a maths test. And another thing that's not supposed to happen in the middle of a maths test is for an alarm clock to go off in someone's bag.

'It's a fire drill!' Larry Franco shouted. 'We should evacuate the building!'

'It's not a fire drill,' Ms Fenwick said. She came swooping up the row where I was sitting and homed in on my bag.

RRRRRRIIIIIINNNNNNGGGGG!

'Stacy, could you please put a stop to that infernal *noise*!' Ms Fenwick said.

That's me: Stacy Allen, once an ordinary ten-year-old student in Four Corners, Indiana. Now, the cause of infernal noises in the middle of a maths test.

'Betsy Jane, what were you yelling about?' Ms Fenwick asked.

'I jabbed my pencil in my eye!' Betsy Jane wailed.

While Ms Fenwick examined Betsy Jane's eye, I hauled my bag up onto my desk and rummaged through my stuff in search of the ringing alarm clock.

There it was. Right at the bottom. It got even louder as I pulled it out and jerked down the lever to shut it off.

'*Thank* you,' Ms Fenwick said. 'Quiet, everyone, please!'

The whole class was talking now and, out of Ms Fenwick's eyesight, a few kids were swapping answers.

Ms Fenwick's eagle-eyes moved around the class and everyone went quiet.

'Well, Stacy?' she said, looking at the alarm clock and then looking at me. 'Would you like to explain why you thought it was a good idea to bring an alarm clock to class?'

Good question.

But did I have a good answer? I sure did, but not one I could tell Ms Fenwick. I knew *exactly* how that alarm clock got into my bag. And it was nothing to do with me, I can tell you that. I *knew* who put it there, and I knew why.

'I must have put it in there by accident,' I said to Ms Fenwick. 'Things like that happen when you're in a hurry,' I added. I looked at my friend Cindy. 'Don't they?'

Cindy gave me a blank look for a second then nodded in agreement. 'They sure do,' she said. 'Last week I brought a tube of toothpaste into school by mistake. I don't know how it got in my bag because I hadn't taken my bag into the bathroom at all that morning.'

'Aliens, I guess,' said Fern, who was sitting right behind us. Just recently Fern has started blaming aliens for anything strange that happens.

A tube of toothpaste appears in your school bag? *Aliens!*

An alarm clock goes off in the middle of a maths test? You got it: *Aliens!*

Bug-eyed monsters from Venus. Except that the bug-eyed monster who put the alarm clock in my bag wasn't from Venus. She was from the bedroom down the hall from mine. It was my big, airheaded bimbo of a sister, Amanda!

I knew *why*. It was her idea of a really great way of getting back at me for slipping one of Sam's pacifiers in with her cheerleading stuff the day before.

But I only did that to pay her back for pinning a *Kick Me* sign onto the back of my sweater the day before that. She *started* it!

Honest, she did! OK, so the *Kick Me* note was to get back at me for taking the laces out of her sneakers. But what would you do if your sister doctored your toothpaste with soap so you came screaming out of the bathroom foaming at the mouth like you had *rabies*?

I'll be honest with you: I don't really remember *who* started all this revenge stuff. But I was pretty determined about who was going to *finish* it.

Me, that's who.

My first reaction was to hunt Amanda down after class and stuff the alarm clock right down her throat. But no; that wouldn't be *nearly* bad enough. What I needed to come up with was something so *sneaky*, so *diabolically* clever that people in our school would be talking about it in twenty years' time.

It would be known as *The Great Revenge*. The day when Stacy finally won over her big sister! Brain over brawn. Not that Amanda's especially brawny, except between the ears.

5

The real problem is that she's a couple of years older than me and behaves like she knows *everything*.

I'll tell you, you could write down everything Amanda knows on the back of a postage stamp, and still leave room for the Gettysburg Address.

Anyway, Ms Fenwick got everyone settled down again and we finished the maths test without anything going off in anyone else's bag. I guess no one else in my class has a crazy older sister like I do.

'Amanda's gone too far this time,' I told my three best friends as we headed back to my house after school. 'I'm going to have to *kill* her. It's the only way the rest of my life is going to be worth living.'

My three best friends are Cindy Spiegel, Fern Kipsak and Pippa Kane. Cindy is my *very* best friend, but usually all four of us hang around together.

What we're like:

Pippa is kind of gangly with long black hair that she almost always wears in a thick braid down her back. She's brainy but totally impractical. And she has the worst *good ideas* in the world. You know the kind of thing I mean. When Pippa says, 'Hey, guys, I've just had a really *good idea*. Why don't we have a

6

picnic in Maynard Park?' you just *know* that within ten minutes of arriving there with all the picnic stuff, there'd be a hurricane, a tornado, an earthquake *and* a plague of locusts.

In fact, just about everything that I'm going to tell you right now happened because I went along with one of Pippa's good ideas. I'll explain about it later.

Cindy is just about the prettiest girl I know. She's already two inches taller than me, and she's got this lovely auburn hair and a fabulous smile. It's a good thing she's my extra special best friend, really, because otherwise I'd be *so* jealous of her! But she's not stuck-up at all, which makes a change from Amanda. Cindy is the nicest, kindest, most thoughtful person I know. We're going to be super-best-friends for the rest of our lives.

Fern is the shortest and the youngest of us, but she's also the noisiest. I wouldn't describe her as scruffy, but she does look kind of *slept-in* sometimes and her hair always seems to be a mess. I really like Fern, even though sometimes she says things that are a little annoying.

Like now.

'I thought it was pretty funny,' Fern said with a grin, meaning Amanda's alarm-clock-in-the-bag routine. 'Did you see the way everyone jumped?' Fern giggled. 'Things like that should happen more often.'

'Oh, right,' I said. 'I'll go tell Amanda to come up with more ways to make me look dumb in front of everyone. As long as *you* think it's funny!'

'Don't get upset,' Fern said. 'It *was* funny. You'd have thought it was funny if the clock had been in someone else's bag.'

'That's not the point,' I said. 'It wasn't in someone else's bag. It was in *my* bag. And Amanda has got to suffer for it!'

'It sure is an escalation,' Pippa said. Pippa's mom is a college professor. That's how come Pippa drops these long words into the conversation every once in a while.

We all looked at her.

'Doesn't that mean a hole in the ground?' Fern asked.

'No, that's an *excavation*,' Pippa said. 'An escalation is like when someone does something to someone else that's a lot worse than anything that the other person has already done to them in the first place.'

Cindy crossed her eyes. 'Thanks for the explanation, Pippa,' she said. 'I understand *perfectly* now.'

'I think I get it,' I said. 'You mean, like I hide a pacifier in Amanda's stuff and she

8

comes back with an alarm clock hidden in my bag and set to go off in the middle of a test.'

'Exactly,' Pippa said. 'That's escalation.'

'So Stacy has got to come up with something even *worse*,' Fern said. She gave me a thoughtful look. 'How about training a giant eagle to swoop down, grab Amanda by the hair, and carry her off in its claws?'

'That's a great idea, Fern,' I said. 'Do you know anywhere I can get a gigantic eagle at short notice?'

'Isn't there a gigantic eagle store in the mall?' Fern said.

'I *wish*!' I sighed. 'I wish there was a store full of useful stuff like that.'

That's exactly the kind of thing a younger sister like me needs. An Anti-Big-Sister Store. Not that Amanda and I are *always* fighting. But when we *do* fight it tends to *escalate* as Pippa would say.

And right now, it was me who had to come up with the perfect *escalation*.

'Oh, hi, Stacy.' I spun around. It was Amanda. She'd come up behind us without a sound. She grinned, lifting her arm and pushing her sleeve back to look at her watch.

'Oh, gee,' she said. 'My watch has stopped. Do you have any idea what time it is, Stacy?'

'Funn-ee!' I said. 'I think it's time you

packed up and left town, because I'm going to get you but good!'

Amanda gave me this really surprised look.

'Why? What's wrong, Stacy? You look kind of *alarmed*.' She burst out laughing and then went running off to catch up with a bunch of her friends before I could think of anything to say back.

Ooh! Amanda Allen, I'm going to *get* you! I'm going to get you if it's the last thing I do!

At least, that was the plan until we all got back to my house and found a letter on the hall table that changed everything.

# Chapter Two

I've been writing to my pen pal Craig for a few months now. He lives in Pennsylvania. His full name is Craig Ralph Newman. He hates the *Ralph* part. He got given that because it was his grandfather's name.

I saw his name and address in the *Letters* page of one of my wildlife magazines. I wrote and told him about a project on whales we'd done at school. He wrote back, telling me about a project his class was doing on endangered species. He also wrote that he was interested in astronomy. And he tried to explain *black holes* to me.

Black holes are these weird things in outer space like huge great vacuum cleaners that kind of *suck* stuff into them. And, according to Craig, anything that goes into a black hole never comes out again. It just disappears. I was reading that part to Mom and she said, 'Just like Amanda's room! Stuff goes in there and never comes out again.'

'What do you mean?' Amanda had said. 'What things?'

'Glasses,' Mom had said, 'plates, bowls, spoons, scissors, pens.'

'OK, OK,' Amanda had said. 'I get the picture.'

'My best letter-writing paper,' Mom had continued. 'The vase from the living room table.'

'I needed it for a still life,' Amanda had said. Amanda's real good at anything artistic. It's the one thing she's really brilliant at.

Anyway, back to that first letter from Craig. You see, the thing was that I hadn't mentioned anything much about myself in my letter, apart from telling him that I went to Four Corners Middle School and was interested in wildlife. But when he wrote back to me, he told me he was twelve, and he sent a picture of himself.

Now I'm not interested in boys *that* way, but Craig looked the kind of boy I *would* be interested in if I *was*. I mean, it's not like I've got some dumb *crush* on him or anything. I don't *do* that sort of thing. The fact that I keep his picture on my bedside table doesn't mean a *thing*, OK?

Where was I? Oh, yeah, the picture. Craig had a really friendly face and a nice smile and curly light brown hair. And on the back of the picture he had written: I am twelve. My birthday is the twentieth of April. When is yours? How about sending me your picture?

Twelve! He was two years older than me. He was more Amanda's age than mine. And he wanted to know what I looked like.

I look like a scrawny ten-year-old. I've got these dopey freckles, and this really *straight* flat, boring brown hair. And I've got braces that I have to wear for two whole years! Would Craig be prepared to wait two years for a picture of me smiling? By then he'd be fourteen and I'd be as skinny and freckly as ever.

I'd shown the letter and the picture to my friends. They all thought Craig looked and sounded really nice.

'So send him your picture,' Fern had said. 'What's the problem?'

'I'm not sure he's going to want to write to a ten-year-old with braces,' I had explained.

'So lie to him about your age,' Fern had said. 'He's not going to know any different.'

'He will if I send him a picture,' I had said. 'There's no way anyone would think I was twelve if they saw a picture of me.'

'Send him a picture of someone else,' Pippa had suggested.

Well, it seemed kind of harmless. I didn't want Craig to give up writing to me because he thought I was just some dorky kid. So I wrote to him and told him I was twelve, too. And I sent him a picture of Amanda.

On the back I wrote. 'This is me. I'm twelve.' And I wrote down my birthday as well.

I guess I should explain something. Amanda and I don't look much like each other. In fact, we look totally different. For a start, Amanda has big blue eyes and naturally wavy blonde hair. And she's . . . I can't say it! It's no good, I just can't say it!

*Go on; it's not going to kill you.*

OK. I'll write it down, but you've got to promise not to read it, OK? Don't read the next line.

Amanda is really, really pretty.

Anyway, what made things worse was that I got a letter back from Craig telling me that he was carrying my picture around with him in his wallet and that all his friends were jealous that he had such a nice-looking pen pal.

'He sounds like he really likes you,' Cindy had said when I'd shown her the letter.

'Yes, but it's not *me*!' I'd pointed out. 'It's *Amanda* that he really likes. Not me!'

'Maybe,' Cindy had said. 'But it's *you* who writes the letters. So it's your *personality* he likes.'

My personality. Amanda's looks.

Oh well, there was nothing I could do about it, not without admitting to Craig that the picture wasn't me at all. I could just imagine what would happen if I did that. And if I sent him a photo of the real me:

*Dear Stacy,*
*Thanks for your really interesting letter, and for letting me know that you are really only ten and that the girl in the first picture was really your big sister, Amanda. Please give her the enclosed letter, because I would like to start writing to her instead of you. Oh, by the way, I think you meant to enclose a picture of yourself with the letter, but you accidentally enclosed a picture of a circus freak. It was nice knowing you. Goodbye,*
*Craig.*

Anyway, back to the present, and the four of us getting to my house after school and finding a letter from Craig.

We all went up to my room and I opened the letter and started reading it out to them.

'Dear Stacy,' I read.

'Hey, original start,' Fern said.

'Are you going to listen, or do you want to keep interrupting?' I asked her.

'I can do both,' Fern said. 'Keep on reading.'

I like Craig's letters. If you read them out loud, you can almost imagine he's in the room talking to you. This letter was mostly about a new project he was doing at school about the Rocky Mountains.

'Some of the animals we're looking at,' I read to the others, 'are grizzly bears, black bears, brown bears, pronghorns, bighorns – '

'*What*horns?' Fern asked.

'Bighorns,' I said.

'No,' Fern said. 'The other ones.'

'Uh . . . pronghorns,' I said.

'What the heck is a pronghorn?' Fern asked.

'He doesn't say,' I said.

'Imagine not knowing what a pronghorn is,' Pippa said.

'OK, brainbox,' Fern said. 'What *is* it?'

'It's an animal,' Pippa said. 'With horns. Kind of *prongy* horns. That's how come it got called a pronghorn. It's closely related to the squirlyhorn, which has squirly kind of horns.'

'Are you making all this up?' Cindy asked. 'I bet there's no such thing as a squirlyhorn. And what does *squirly* mean, anyhow?'

'It's a cross between whirly and square,' Pippa said.

'Don't believe her,' Fern said. 'She's making it up.' She looked at me. 'What else does Craig say? Anything interesting?'

'It's all interesting,' I said.

'Yeah, but only if you're a wildlife nut,' Fern said. 'Is there anything in there that a *normal* person would find interesting?'

I read a few more paragraphs about the Rockies and then a piece about what stars he could see right then in the night sky. I've got to admit, I'd never thought about astronomy, but somehow Craig made it sound really interesting.

'Oh, yes,' I read, 'I've got some really good news. My parents are taking a trip to Indiana one Saturday soon. They aren't going to be far from where you live. They said I can come with them, and they'll put me on a train to Four Corners. I'll be able to spend the day there! How's that, huh? Here's my phone number. Give me a call and we can make some plans.' I stopped reading as my mouth fell open.

'That'll be nice,' Cindy said. 'You'll be able to meet him at last.'

'Yes, but, no, but – *wait*!' I stammered. 'He can't. I can't. We *can't*! We can't meet up. He'll see I'm not me. I mean, he'll see I'm not who I said I was. He'll know I pretended to be Amanda. What am I going to *do*?'

Pippa shook her head. 'That's what happens

17

when you start telling fibs to people,' she said. 'You *always* get found out.'

'What!' I yelled. 'It was your idea to send him a picture of Amanda.'

'No, it wasn't,' Pippa said.

'Oh, yes it was,' Cindy and Fern said together.

'Only because you were panicking about him not wanting to write to you if he thought you looked like you,' Pippa said. 'It was just an idea. I never said I thought it was a *good* idea.'

'Since when have any of your ideas been *good* ideas?' I said. 'Your ideas are always terrible. And this has got to be the worst of the whole bunch! For heaven's sake, he's coming *here* next month. What am I going to do, you guys?'

'Well,' Pippa began, 'if you ask me – '

'Not you!' I said. 'You've already gotten me in enough trouble. Just keep quiet!'

'Charming,' Pippa said. 'If that's how you feel, I think I'll go home. You obviously don't need *me* around messing your life up.' She stood up and picked up her bag.

'Oh, come on, Pippa. Don't be like that,' I said.

'I'm not being like anything,' Pippa said. 'If anyone's being like anything, then it isn't me.

18

It's *you*! I'll see you tomorrow. But don't worry, I won't say a word! I wouldn't want to get you into any more trouble.'

Cindy and Fern sat on the carpet looking kind of awkward as Pippa walked out. I guess I should have gone right after her, but I was still in a panic about Craig. And it *had* been Pippa's idea to send him that picture of Amanda, no matter what she said.

'Wow,' Cindy breathed as we heard the front door slam. 'You've really upset her, Stacy.'

'But she does have bad ideas,' I said. 'Doesn't she, guys? You *know* she does.'

'But that's just Pippa,' Fern said.

'You didn't have to send that picture of Amanda just because Pippa suggested it,' Cindy said reasonably.

'OK,' I sighed. 'I know, I know. I'll make up with her. I'll phone her later. But meanwhile, what am I going to do about Craig?'

# Chapter Three

'Hi, Mrs Kane. Is Pippa there, please?' I was sitting on the stairs with the phone. It was just after dinner that same day.

I waited for Pippa to come to the phone. I twiddled the cord nervously. I'd never had a real argument with Pippa before and I was kind of worried that she might just hang up on me once she knew who it was.

'Hello?' It was Pippa's voice.

'Hi, it's me,' I said, trying to sound all happy and cheerful and pleased to be speaking to her.

'Hello, me.'

'How's things?' I asked.

'Fine.' Did she sound annoyed? I wasn't sure. It's difficult to tell when a person isn't saying very much to you.

'Cindy and Fern went home a little while after you left,' I said.

'Uh-huh,' Pippa said.

'We didn't come up with any ideas about

Craig,' I said. 'Well, Fern came up with one idea. She said I should write him pretending to be my mom and tell him that I'd been kidnapped by aliens. You know. "Dear Craig, Thank you for your letter to my daughter, Stacy. I'm afraid there's no point in you coming to visit, as she was abducted by aliens on Tuesday on her way home from school." '

'That sounds like Fern,' Pippa said.

'Hey, Pippa?' I said. 'I'm really sorry I was nasty to you.'

'You were right, though,' Pippa sighed. 'I always *do* have terrible ideas. I don't know why. They always seem like good ideas when I have them, but something goes screwy every time.'

'Not *every* time,' I said. 'Sometimes your ideas work out fine.'

'Like when?' Pippa asked.

'Uh . . .'

'See!' Pippa said. 'Face it, Stacy, I'm a disaster area. I always have been. My very first memory is of blowing the oven up in the kitchen when I was about four years old.'

'You did?' I said. I was pretty impressed. Four years old and causing explosions already.

'Yeah,' Pippa said. 'We had a dog. It was before my mom and dad split up. I thought the dog would want some hot food for a change so

21

I put an unopened can of dog food in the oven.' Pippa sighed. 'It blew the oven door right off its hinges.'

I tried not to giggle. 'Oh, Pippa!'

'And now I've caused you all this trouble with your pen pal,' Pippa said. 'You should never, never listen to me, Stacy. I ought to have a warning notice glued to my forehead. "Taking this girl's advice can seriously damage your health." I don't blame you for being annoyed with me.'

'That's just silly,' I said. 'I'm not annoyed with you. I thought you were annoyed with me.'

'Only because you were right,' Pippa said. 'It was my fault that you sent that picture of Amanda.'

'That doesn't matter now,' I said. 'What we need to come up with now is some way of keeping Craig away. Unfortunately.'

'Why *unfortunately*?' Pippa asked.

'I'd like to have met him,' I said. 'I think he's really nice.'

'Ooh! Stacy's got a crush on Craig!' Pippa sang down the phone.

'I do *not*,' I yelled. 'Can't a person say she likes another person without people making dumb comments?'

22

'Sorr-ee!' Pippa said. 'You're kind of touchy about it, Stacy.'

'I am not,' I said. I wanted to change the subject. I was glad Pippa couldn't see how much I was blushing. 'Anyway,' I said, 'to get back to the point: how do we keep Craig from coming here?'

'Didn't Fern or Cindy come up with anything?' Pippa asked.

'I already told you Fern's idea.'

'Oh, yeah. Aliens,' Pippa said. 'What about Cindy?'

'She said I should write and tell him I'm sick,' I said. 'But he wants me to call him, that's the problem. Not only do I have to sound *sick*, I'll have to sound twelve-years-old, too. Do I sound twelve to you on the phone?'

'I don't know,' Pippa said. 'What does twelve sound like?'

'Kind of like Amanda, I guess,' I said. 'She's thirteen, but only *just* thirteen. Do I sound anything like Amanda on the phone?'

'I don't really know. I haven't spoken to Amanda on the phone much. I don't remember what she sounds like.'

'Wait a minute,' I said. I put my hand over the mouthpiece. 'Amanda!' I yelled up the stairs.

'What?' came the reply from Amanda's room.

'Phone!'

There was a stamping of feet in the hallway and Amanda appeared at the top of the stairs. I held the phone up for her.

'I didn't hear it ring,' she said as she sat halfway down the stairs and took the receiver from me. 'Hi,' she said into the phone.

Her face went blank. She took the phone away from her ear and stared at it. Then she stared at me. Then she spoke into the receiver. 'Who the heck is this? No, I will not recite *Mary Had a Little Lamb*. Is this supposed to be funny? What? What?'

She shook her head and held the phone out to me. 'It's your friend Pippa,' she said. 'It's not for me at all. What's the matter with you?'

'I know it's Pippa,' I said. 'We were trying to find out if I sound like you on the phone.' I took the receiver from her and spoke into it. 'Well? Do I sound like Amanda?'

'Not really,' Pippa said. 'But I don't know if you sound younger or just different.'

'You dragged me all the way down here just to see if you sound like me on the phone?' Amanda demanded. 'What kind of a nut are you?'

'It was important,' I told Amanda.

'What?' Pippa said.

'I was talking to Amanda,' I said into the phone.

'I think you'd better hang up, Stacy,' Amanda said. 'I need to call the funny farm. You need specialist treatment.'

Pippa said something I didn't hear.

'What did you say?' I asked.

'I said you need your head looking at!' Amanda yelled.

'I wasn't talking to you,' I said. 'I was talking to Pippa. What did you say just then, Pippa?'

'I said, what did Amanda say,' Pippa said.

'What did she say?' Amanda demanded. 'Did she say something bad about me?'

'No!' I hollered. 'Will you just shut up for a moment?'

'Who? Me?' Pippa asked.

'Of all the – ' Amanda began.

'What on earth is going on out here?' Dad stuck his head out of the living room doorway. 'We can't hear ourselves think. Keep it down to a roar, please!'

'I'll see you in the morning,' I told Pippa. I quickly put the phone down and gave Dad a big innocent smile. 'All over,' I said. 'Sorry about the noise.'

Dad's head vanished back into the living room.

'I ought to scoop your head out and use it as a fish bowl!' Amanda said. 'You're getting *worse*, Stacy. Do you know that?' She got up and stamped upstairs.

Now I guess I could have just explained the whole thing to Amanda right there and then, but I had the sneaky feeling that it might *damage* her if I told her I'd sent a picture of her to my pen pal, pretending it was me. I mean, she might *hurt* herself laughing.

I followed her upstairs.

'Hey, Amanda,' I said, 'you know all about boys, don't you?'

She gave me one of her suspicious looks. 'What's that supposed to mean?' she asked. 'Is this going to be one of your feeb jokes?'

'Not at all,' I said. 'It's just that . . .' Come on, Stacy, *think*. It's just that *what*? Ding! A lightbulb went on in my head.

'It's just that Pippa is being pestered by this boy,' I said. 'She needs someone with lots of experience with boys to give her some advice on how to get rid of him.'

Amanda laughed. 'With a face like hers she won't need any other help. Does this boy need glasses, or what?'

I took a deep breath. Mom taught me to do that. When someone says something that gets you mad, take a deep breath and count to ten.

26

While I was still counting, Amanda went into her room and slammed the door in my face.

So much for Mom's brilliant ideas!

I knocked on Amanda's door and went into her room.

'I was talking to you,' I said. 'Hey, come on, Amanda. You know all about boys. What should Pippa do?' Amanda sat on the pillows on her floor and picked up the magazine she'd obviously been reading when I'd called her to the phone.

'Tell her to write to an advice column,' Amanda said, sprawling on her front and flicking through the magazine.

'Oh, I get it,' I said. 'You don't *know* what she should do. Hey, sorry I bothered you, Amanda.' I headed for the door.

'Just a minute,' Amanda said. 'Who says I don't know?'

I turned around and looked at her. I knew that would get her. 'Do you?' I asked.

She sat up. 'What exactly is Pippa's problem?'

I sat on the edge of her bed. 'Well,' I said, 'there's this boy, you see . . . uh, and he wants to ask her out, right? But she doesn't want to go out with him. But she doesn't want to upset him either. So she needs to come up with

27

some way of sort of putting him off without being unkind. What would you do?'

Amanda looked thoughtful. The problem with Amanda is that it takes her so much effort to *look* thoughtful, that it doesn't leave her much room to do any actual *thinking*.

'She could tell him to hit the road or her big brother will go around to his house and rearrange his teeth for him,' Amanda said.

'I'm not sure that's what she had in mind,' I said. 'She doesn't want to upset him, so I don't think she's going to want to threaten him with a punch in the mouth. Can't you think of anything more friendly?'

'How about a really bad cold?' Amanda suggested.

'Yea-ah, I gue-ess,' I said.

'Or she could always invite him to her place and then get him to help her with some really boring chores,' Amanda said. 'That'd get rid of him.' Her eyes lit up. 'Or she could pretend she's crazy in love with him. She could tell him she dreams about him every night. She could tell him she counts the seconds when they're not together. She could tell him she wants to spend the whole of the rest of her life with him.' Amanda grinned. 'She could tell him she wants to get *engaged*! If that doesn't frighten him to death, I don't know what would.'

So far, none of Amanda's ideas came even *close*. Except for the one about the bad cold, I guess. If I shoved some tissues up my nose and talked really hoarsely when I called him, maybe he wouldn't be able to make out that I was only ten.

But the problem with that was that it was pretty obvious from his letter that he wanted me to call him up in the next few days. So I'd have to have my terrible cold right now. But he wasn't coming to visit for another couple of weeks. I mean, just how bad a cold was I going to have to be suffering from?

'Hi, Craig, I'b sorry bud I ca'd beed you negst Saddurday becob I'b godd a bad head code. Yeah, ib's one ob dose codes dad lasds for two weegs ad leasd. Pobbably logger.'

No, a cold wasn't the answer. But I needed to come up with *something* pretty quickly.

Even if it was only a Pippa-type idea. At least that would be something. And what I didn't realize right then was that my time was running out a whole lot quicker than I knew.

# Chapter Four

The next morning before school started I met Cindy in the corridor outside our classroom.

'Amanda's ideas about keeping Craig away were all pretty useless,' I told her.

'Did you tell her the whole story?' Cindy asked. 'About her picture and everything?'

'No way! Do you think I'm crazy?' Even the *thought* of admitting something like that to Amanda gave me the shudders. I mean, I might as well broadcast it over the school public address system.

'Ahem! Could I have all your attention, please, students. This is an official announcement. Stacy Allen would like everyone to know that she wishes she was as pretty as her sister. Did everyone get that? Stacy Allen is totally and completely jealous of her sister, Amanda.'

Hmm. Sure!

'I've been thinking,' Cindy said. 'Do you remember Barton MacKenzie?'

Barton MacKenzie was a kid who went to

our school until his folks moved to Alaska or something. All I could remember about him was that he sniffed all the time and *did* things with his nose.

'I wish I didn't,' I said. 'Why?'

'He asked me out to a party last summer,' Cindy said. 'And I got out of going with him by telling him he brought me out in a rash.'

I looked at Cindy. Barton MacKenzie was enough to give a warthog a rash. What I couldn't figure was why Cindy was telling me this.

'So are you saying I should tell Craig I can't meet him because he brings me out in a rash?' I said. 'What kind of rash? A letter rash? A rash from his *writing*?'

Cindy shook her head sadly. 'No, I guess that wouldn't work,' she said. 'That's a shame. When you've actually met someone it's a lot easier to come up with reasons for avoiding them.' She gave a sniff, crossed her eyes and backed away from me. 'Ew! You smell *bad*!' she said. 'Get *away* from me before I get sick!'

'Cindy Spiegel! What a terrible thing to say!' We both jumped. It was Ms Fenwick. We hadn't heard her come up behind us.

Cindy went bright red. 'I was only fooling,' she said. 'I didn't mean it. Stacy doesn't smell at all.'

31

Ms Fenwick gave her a disapproving frown as she walked past into the classroom.

'Oh, heck,' Cindy muttered. 'Now she's going to think I'm some awful kind of person. And I was only trying to think of the type of things you could say to get rid of someone you don't like.'

'But I do like Craig,' I reminded her. 'I like him a *lot*. That's the whole point. I've got to come up with some way of getting rid of him without . . . well, without *getting rid of him*, if you see what I mean.'

'Hi, guys!' It was Fern and Pippa.

Pippa and I looked at each other and smiled, and I think we both knew right away that everything was OK between us again.

'I've just been totally embarrassed in front of Ms Fenwick,' Cindy said. 'We're still trying to come up with ways for Stacy to get out of meeting Craig.'

'How about you arrange to meet him somewhere and then just don't show up?' Fern said. 'Simple, easy and clean. And then afterwards you apologize. You can tell him you were delayed or you were sick or you had to look after Sam because your mom and dad had been carried off by . . .'

'Aliens!' we chorused.

Fern grinned. 'Exactly!' she said.

'And what if Craig calls my house to ask where I am?' I said.

'What if he goes round to your house to look for you?' Cindy said. 'And *Amanda* opens the door.'

'Don't even think about it!' I said. 'Look, guys, I'm supposed to call him in the next day or two. We've got to come up with some good ideas – fast.'

'Does that include me?' Pippa asked.

I gave her a big smile. 'Of course,' I said.

'Well, I did have one idea.' Pippa shook her head. 'No, you'll think it's dumb. Forget it.'

'We won't think it's dumb,' said Cindy.

'Don't bet on it,' Fern mumbled.

'There!' Pippa said. 'Fern already thinks it's dumb and she hasn't even heard it yet. I'm not going to open my mouth again!'

And she meant it. We couldn't get a word out of her until lunchtime, even though Fern apologized and Cindy and I did our best to get her to tell us her idea.

It wasn't until we were in the cafeteria at our favourite table that Fern finally came up with a way of getting Pippa to tell us her idea.

'See this yoghurt?' Fern said, holding a pot of strawberry yoghurt under Pippa's nose. 'If you don't tell us what your idea was by the time I've counted to three, you're going to be wearing it.'

'You wouldn't,' Pippa said.

'One . . .' Fern said.

'You don't fool me,' Pippa said.

'Two . . .' Fern lifted the pot so it was hovering above Pippa's head. Pippa's eyes rolled up to follow it.

'You won't,' Pippa said uneasily.

'She will,' Cindy said. 'You'd better believe it.'

'Thr – '

'OK, OK, I'll tell you,' Pippa said. 'I just thought that maybe Stacy could dress up to look like Amanda.' Pippa looked around at us. We were all sitting there with completely blank faces.

'That was *it*?' Fern said. 'That was the great idea you've been keeping us in suspense about all morning? Stacy dressing up to look like Amanda? Hey, why not go all the way, while you're at it? Why not have her dress up like Marilyn Monroe? I mean, why stop with Amanda?'

'I said you'd think it was dumb,' Pippa mumbled. 'That's why I didn't want to tell you.'

'At least there's one good thing about it,' I said. 'It's *so* dumb that we don't even have to worry about it going wrong.' I looked at Pippa. 'I mean, come on, not in a million years am I going to be able to dress up so I look like Amanda. I'm too short.'

'You could wear platform shoes,' Pippa said.

'I'd need stilts!' I said. 'And my hair's the wrong colour. Have you looked at Amanda recently? Like, have you noticed anything about the colour of her *hair*? She's blonde, Pippa. And my hair is brown.'

'You could wear a wig,' Pippa said.

'I have braces!' I almost yelled. 'Amanda is grinning like the Cheshire Cat in the picture I sent. You can see almost every tooth in her entire head! How am I supposed to explain that?'

'Just don't open your mouth while you're with Craig,' Fern said.

'And how do I *talk* to him?' I asked. 'Like a ventriloquist.' I put on a fixed slitty grin so my lips were hardly open. 'Hi, Graig, I'g Stacy. Gleased to geet gou.' I shook my head. 'I can't believe we are actually *discussing* this as if it's even a possibility. There is no way, no way at all, that I am going to meet up with Craig disguised to look like Amanda. Period! End of conversation!'

\* \* \*

I haven't really introduced the rest of my family yet, have I? I guess this is a good place to do it, especially as my mom was directly involved in the next major disaster in my life.

Although you wouldn't know it from the way Amanda thinks she *owns* our house, there are actually six of us living there. There's Amanda (who you've met), and there's me, and there's my cat, Benjamin. He's a Russian Blue and he's my absolute best male friend, despite the fact that he keeps giving me heart attacks by climbing up on the roof to chase birds.

Then there's the new addition to the Allen family. Baby Sam. He was kind of a surprise all round, but Mom says she's always loved surprises, and she loves Sam most of all. We all do. It's the one thing that Amanda and I never disagree about. Sam is just too perfect to be true!

Then there's my dad. Dad's job is selling books. Not to ordinary people, but to bookstores. He works mostly up in the north-east part of the state up near Lake Michigan. The big problem is that Dad's job means that sometimes he has to be away from home for a few nights in a row. But when that happens he calls home every evening.

Dad might work a long way off, but Mom

sure doesn't. Mom works in our basement! It's true. Our basement has been converted into an office. Mom works as a proofreader for these huge, mega-boring manuscripts. She also makes some money on the side by writing rhymes to go in greetings cards.

Mom doesn't always have Sam with her when she's working, not if there's someone else around to keep an eye on him. Speaking of which, I guess that's the only thing about Sam that Amanda and I ever argue about. Somehow, and I don't know *how*, Amanda always seems to be too busy to look after Sam. Either she's got a little socializing to do, or she's got to go to a cheerleading practice, or she's got some *other* good excuse for having to be out of the house right when Sam needs looking after.

Take that afternoon. After school my friends and I went over to Fern's house for a while to say hello to our temporary dog, Hobo, and her puppies. Hobo's story is kind of complicated. Fern found Hobo just before she had her puppies, but just after the pups were born, the owners found out where Hobo was and wanted her back. But Fern is looking after Hobo and the puppies until they're twelve weeks old.

Hobo is really called Sapphire, but we still

call her Hobo while she's with us. The Burtons, who actually own Hobo/Sapphire, are going to let us keep a puppy. We've named him Lucky Eddie Quasimodo Paddle-Steamer Hawkeye Lafayette Kipsak-Spiegel-Allen-Kane the First. I don't have time right now to explain how he got such a long name. Anyway, we call him Lucky for short.

I got home to find Amanda sitting on the couch playing with Sam.

'Oh, great,' she said. 'You're here.' She got up. 'I've got to go meet Rachel. Mom says will you keep an eye on Sam for an hour or so? She's finishing some stuff up downstairs.'

See what I mean about Amanda?

'Hey, hold on,' I said. 'I just walked in the *door*.'

'Sorry,' Amanda said, sweeping past me as she headed for the great outdoors. 'No time to stand around talking. See you!'

'Well, I – '

'Oh,' Amanda interrupted. 'There was a phone call for you. Mom answered it. Byee-ee.' Slam!

Oooh! One of these *days*, Amanda . . .

I picked Sam up and went down to the basement.

Mom was sitting at her word processor, typing up a storm. Mom is funny when she concentrates. She sticks her tongue out and kind of curls it up as though she's trying to polish the end of her nose with it.

'What is it, honey?' She asked without turning around. 'I'm really busy just now.' Her fingers were still zooming over the keyboard.

'Amanda said there was a call for me,' I said.

'Oh, yeah,' Mom said. 'It was from your pen pal. From Craig.' My stomach went: whoopgrungle-*ker-thunk*! 'I wrote the message down somewhere,' Mom continued. 'He said his folks will be in Indianapolis the week after next and he'll be able to come over to visit for a few hours during the afternoon.' Mom turned and smiled at me. 'Won't that be great?' she said. 'I told him I *knew* you'd really be looking forward to seeing him. He wants you to call back as soon as you can to sort out the details. Stacy, are you OK? You look a little pale. Don't you feel well?'

'Me?' I said with a sickly little laugh. 'No, I feel . . . just . . . fine . . .'

Actually, I felt like going: AAAAAARRR-RGGGGGHHHHH!!!!!

# Chapter Five

*Have you ever found that you are bored by all the regular ice cream flavours available at your local supermarket?*

*Do you ever find yourself hankering after something just that little bit different?*

*If the answer to that question is 'Yes' then why don't you come on down to Captain Scoop's Ocean Ice Cream Emporium where our trained staff will introduce your tired tastebuds to our new range of Fish-Flavoured Ice Cream!*

*Double Cod-Chocolate Chip.*

*Mackerel Surprise.*

*Turbot and Shrimp Ripple.*

*Herring Neopolitan.*

*And the ever-popular Tuna and Cream Supreme.*

*Mmmm! Sounds delicious, huh? Do yourself a favour come on down to Captain Scoop's! Ice Cream will never be the same again!*

Yuck! Don't some *strange* things pop into your head when you're in shock?

Now. Where was I? My mind had gone completely blank.

Oh, yes. I remember! AAAARRRRGGG-GHHHH!!!!

My mom had spoken to Craig on the phone and she'd told him I'd be delighted to see him.

Arrrgh!

I was supposed to call him back *as soon as I can* to sort out the details.

Arrrgh!

*What am I going to do???*

I mean, how long can you stand in the middle of your bedroom going *Arrgh*? Sooner or later, *Arrgh*! just isn't enough anymore.

'Mirrow,' Benjamin said as he came slinking through my almost-closed bedroom door to see what was up.

'Oh, hi, honey,' I said, kneeling down so he could pad all over me and rub himself up against me. His tail went *schwoop* across my nose and he started to purr.

I lifted him up and gave him a serious hug.

'Benjamin,' I told him, 'we're in trouble.'

'Broop, mrrp.'

Which is cat for 'Tell me all about it; maybe I can help.' (Huh! Like *heck* it is! It's probably cat for 'Shut up and keep petting me.')

'You know what Mom always tells me?' I said. 'If you tell one lie, you always have to tell

41

another. And then another. And then another, until you get so tangled in them that you don't know which way is up.' I sighed. 'And then you get caught! Well, I think I'm about to be caught in a kind of lie. And it's going to make me look like such an idiot!'

'Brrrrmmm, mrrrrp, brrrmmmm,' Benjamin said as he pounded my legs with his paws and started going around in tight little circles.

I knew what that meant. That meant he was settling down for the night. It meant that if I didn't shift myself within the next few seconds, I was going to be a cat bed for the next two hours.

'Sorry, boy,' I said, gently scooping him out of my lap. 'I've got things to do.'

He gave me a really annoyed look and marched straight under the bed. Sheesh! That cat is one big sulker if he doesn't get what he wants.

I peered under the bed and saw these big glowing eyes staring out at me.

I went into Mom and Dad's room to use the phone. I didn't want to risk Mom coming up out of the basement and hearing what I was going to be talking about.

'Hi, Mrs Spiegel,' I said as a voice answered. 'It's Stacy. Could I speak to Cindy, please?'

Whenever I've been in real trouble and

haven't been able to think of a way out, Cindy, my best friend in the entire world, has always been there to help me.

'Hi, Stacy.' Ahh! Cindy! My saviour!

I told her what had happened.

'Oh, my gosh!' Cindy wailed down the phone. 'That's terrible! What are you going to do?'

'That's what I was hoping you'd tell me,' I said.

'Stacy, it's awful! He's going to turn up at your house and it'll be a total *disaster*!'

'Cindy,' I said, 'this is *not* what I need to hear right now.'

'But he'll know you lied to him,' Cindy said. 'He'll probably think you're a total and utter nerd! Oh, Stacy, what on earth are you going to do!'

'Don't panic,' I said. 'I'll think of something. I'll see you tomorrow, OK?'

'OK, but call me back the second you think of anything,' Cindy said.

'Sure thing,' I said. I put the phone down. *Strike one*!

Well, thanks, Cindy, that was a big help. I called her up to help me. How come I ended up having to calm *her* down?

Hey, wait, though. I know someone who

never panics. Fern never panics. Fern always stays calm and cool and laid-back.

Well, I was right about one thing. Fern didn't panic. She was too busy laughing her *head* off to panic.

'This isn't funny!' I hollered into the phone. I could hear her shrieking with laughter. She was probably rolling on her back in the hall and kicking her legs in the air.

Mental note: People not to phone when you have an embarrassing problem that's about to blow up in your face:

1) *Cindy Spiegel*
2) *Fern Kipsak*

'I'll see you in the morning,' I yelled through all the howls of laughter that were coming out of the phone. 'If you've recovered by then!'

I hung up. *Strike two*!

Who did that leave? Who could I call who wouldn't panic and who *especially* wouldn't laugh? Who was *left* for me to trust with this? Santa Claus? The tooth fairy? The Jolly Green Giant? Pippa?

No. No way. She'd already come up with one idea that was so dumb it would win the gold medal in the Dumb Olympics.

I picked the phone up again.

*No way are you going to call Pippa. It would just be a total waste of time.*

Will you shut up, brain? Can't you see I'm busy?

I pressed out the number.

*This is a waste of time. Hello? Are you listening to me? This is your brain speaking. Read my lips: this is a waste of time! You are wasting your time calling Pippa Kane. You know what will happen. Pippa will come up with something so crazy that it'll come with its own straightjacket.*

'Oh, hi, Pippa. It's Stacy.'

*OK, that's it. Just don't say I didn't warn you.*

'Hi, Stacy. How's things?' Pippa asked.

'I need some help, Pippa,' I said. 'The Craig thing just got a little more complicated.'

*Slam!*

Did you hear that? That was the sound of my brain walking out of my head in disgust. Oh, well, I guess I was on my *own* from now on.

★  ★  ★

'This is crazy,' I said. I looked in the mirror. Something weird and freaky looked back at me. I don't know what it was, but it sure wasn't *me*.

'We're not through yet,' Pippa said. 'I told you not to look until we're finished.'

It was the following afternoon. The four of

us were in my bedroom. I was sitting on the floor while Cindy and Pippa worked on me.

Fern was sitting on the chair by my desk, stroking Benjamin and watching the Great Transformation.

Cindy was putting make-up on me while Pippa fussed around brushing out a blonde wig she'd borrowed from her mother. (Pippa's mother is not the sort of person who goes around in a blonde wig. She used to do amateur dramatics and she still had a trunk of dressing-up stuff left over.)

It felt like Cindy had been painting my face for a couple of hours. Every now and then she'd sit back on her heels, tip her head to one side and click her tongue. Then she'd shake her head, rub at the part of my face she'd been working on with a tissue, and start again.

In her lap was a picture of Amanda that we'd taken from the table in the living room. Cindy looked at it then looked at me. Then she sighed, rubbed at my face with a tissue and got back to work.

The mirror came from the bathroom. Cindy kept turning my face away from it, so I had to strain my eyes almost around to my ears to see what I looked like.

'Well?' I said. 'Are you through yet? Are you going to admit defeat now, or what?'

46

'It's not so bad,' Cindy said, rubbing some more stuff into my cheeks. 'I've almost gotten rid of your freckles.'

'Yup,' Fern said with a grin. 'Another quarter of an inch of that stuff and you won't be able to see them at all.'

'Will you stop criticizing?' Pippa said as she worked on brushing out the last few tangles in the blonde wig. She gave a big tug of the brush and the wig slipped over one eye.

'Pippa!' Cindy said. 'Careful!'

'Aren't you finished yet?' Pippa asked. 'They don't take this long to paint the Golden Gate Bridge.'

'The Golden Gate Bridge doesn't keep *moving*,' Cindy said.

A couple of minutes later Cindy was finished.

'OK, stand up,' Pippa said, 'and we'll put the skirt and T-shirt on you.'

We'd taken some of Amanda's clothes from the laundry basket. Fern was all for us borrowing some stuff from her closet, but I'd made *that* mistake before. It was a whole lot safer just to sneak something out of the laundry. And it didn't smell, or anything. Amanda changes her clothes about every ten seconds. They don't even get the chance to get *warm*, let alone dirty.

'OK,' Cindy said, backing away from me, 'let's take a real good look.' Pippa came in behind her on one side and Fern stood on the other side.

Three pairs of eyes stared at me.

'Well?' I said. 'What's the verdict, guys?'

There was a long, lo-ong pause.

# Chapter Six

'Will someone please *say* something?' I said. 'How do I look?'

'Umm . . .' Pippa mumbled.

'Er . . .' Cindy added.

'We're speechless,' Fern said.

I frowned at them. 'Give me that mirror,' I said. Fern had turned the mirror away so I couldn't see myself anymore. She picked it up from where it was resting against my desk and turned it so I could see what they'd done to me.

I looked as though my face had been dipped in some kind of orange paint. Sure, you couldn't see my freckles. Cindy had plastered the make-up on so thick you could hardly see my *nose*! And I had these huge great bright red lips. And the left hand side of my top lip went up higher than the other side so I looked like I had this permanent sneer. And I had so much make-up around my eyes that I looked like a panda. And Cindy had slapped these great thick red cheekbone lines down either side of my face. I'm telling you, I looked like I was ready to go on the warpath.

An Apache squaw. An Apache squaw known as Face Like A Sat-on Quiche.

And perched on top of this disaster and hanging down either side of that *thing* that used to be my face was Pippa's mom's wig.

It looked like it had fallen out of the sky and just *died* on my head. It wasn't even the same colour as Amanda's hair. It was a kind of grimy straw colour with peculiar-looking brownish highlights.

But let's not forget the clothes. Amanda's T-shirt hung on me like a wrinkly old sack. And her skirt was slipping down over my hips already, even though Pippa had yanked the belt up as tight as she could.

'Maybe if you wore a big coat and stood in the shadows,' Fern said helpfully.

'I look awful!' I said. I didn't yell. I didn't scream or shout or go into a complete panic. What was the point?

'Give me a few more minutes,' Cindy said. 'I can see where it needs a little more work.'

'Yeah,' Fern murmured. 'A head transplant would help for a start.'

'Fern!' Cindy said. 'I wish you wouldn't just stand there making stupid jokes.'

'Jokes?' Fern said, shaking her head. 'Who's making jokes?'

Even Benjamin was staring at me like I'd transformed into some kind of monster.

'Let's forget this,' I said. 'It was a bad idea from the start. We gave it a shot, but there's no way it was ever going to work.' I didn't feel especially disappointed. Heck, I never expected it to work. I'd only gone along with the whole dumb idea to humour Pippa.

'So what are you going to do?' asked Cindy.

'I'm going to go to the bathroom and wash all this mess off, that's what I'm going to do,' I said. 'And then I'm going to move to Canada.'

Cindy looked puzzled. 'I don't get it,' she said. 'Putting make-up on looks so easy when my mom does it. I don't know how Stacy ended up looking so . . . so . . .'

'Ridiculous?' Pippa said with a giggle.

'Bizarre?' Fern added with a laugh.

'Hideous?' I said, grinning a big bright red grin.

Cindy spluttered with laughter. 'Oh, I'm sorry, Stacy. I did my best. Honest, I did.'

'You look like a mutant from another planet,' Pippa laughed. 'You look like one of Fern's aliens.'

I did a wobbly kind of stiff-legged march

towards Fern with my arms stretched out. 'Beep! Beep! Take me to your leader!'

Benjamin took one look as I headed in his direction, stared at me in sheer panic, and bolted for the door.

'Benjy!' I called after him. 'Benjy! It's me. It's only me.'

I ran over to the door. Benjamin's tail was just disappearing down the stairs. I ran after him. I was almost at the bottom of the stairs when I heard the key in the lock of the front door.

Eek! Someone was coming in. I forgot about Benjamin, did a quick about-face on the stairs and tried to zoom back to the safety of my room. But Amanda's skirt chose that moment to finally come properly loose. It went flapping down around my knees and I caught a foot in the hem.

The very next thing I knew, I was flat on my Girl-from-Mars face on the stairs.

'Stacy?'

It was Amanda.

'Mom wants you in the kitchen, right *now*!' I said without looking around.

'Is that my skirt?' Amanda said.

'No.'

'Sure it is. I put it in the wash last night,' Amanda said. 'What the heck are you up to,

Stacy? And what's that you've got on your *head*?'

'Nothing,' I whimpered as I tried to scramble my way up the stairs without letting Amanda get a better look at me.

'That's my T-shirt, too,' Amanda said. 'What's the big idea?' She grabbed my ankle just as I was about to zoom out of sight. She gave a pull and I turned and bounced down a couple of steps on my backside.

'Ouch!' I yelled. 'Be careful!'

Amanda stared at my face. Her eyes opened so wide I was half-afraid they were going to pop right out and land in my lap.

I sat up, tugging at the trailing skirt with one hand and pushing my off-centre wig back in place with the other.

'What's your problem?' I said with all the dignity I could muster. 'Haven't you ever seen a fashion model before?'

'A fashion model?' Amanda gasped. 'Stacy, you look like a road crash! And where did you get that make-up?'

'Cindy brought it over.'

'Over from where? A circus? And what's with the wig?' Suddenly the astonished expression on Amanda's face gave way to something a little more suspicious. 'And why are you wearing *my* clothes?' she asked.

'Well . . .' I began, speaking slowly to give myself time to think of some reasonable story. 'I can see how it might look a little weird, but there's a perfectly good explanation, if you'll just give me a couple of seconds.'

'A couple of seconds to do what?' Amanda asked.

I gave her a bright red smile. 'To think up a perfectly good explanation, of course.'

'Hey!' It was Fern's voice from upstairs. 'Hey, Amanda-monster? Have you – oops!' Her head appeared around the banister. She took one look at Amanda and vanished.

Amanda grabbed hold of the front of the T-shirt.

'What did she mean by that?' she snarled through gritted teeth.

'Careful,' I said. 'Don't crease the merchandise.'

'Is *this* supposed to look like *me*?' Amanda howled.

I managed to squirm out of her grip and dive for the top of the stairs.

'We tried,' I yelled back as I scooted around the banister and headed for my room. 'But we just couldn't make me ugly enough!'

I slammed the door closed and locked it.

Amanda stood and yelled outside the door

for a little while before giving it a good kick
and stamping off to her own room.

I looked at my friends. 'So?' I said. 'What
do we do now?'

There was a short silence.

'I've had another idea,' Pippa said.

★   ★   ★

'Go to Jail,' Cindy said. 'That's the *third* time!'
She picked her piece up from the Monopoly
board and set it down again in Jail.

'That's what comes from being a no-good
low-life hoodlum,' Fern said as she threw the
dice and landed on Fifth Avenue. 'Whoo-ee!'
she said. 'I'll buy *that*.'

'Hey? Guys?' came a muffled voice from
inside my closet. 'Can I come out now? Guys?'

'My turn,' I said, rattling the dice and sending them skidding over the board. I got a
seven. I moved my piece to Community Chest
and picked up the next card.

I almost choked laughing.

' "You have won second prize in a beauty
contest. Receive fifty dollars".'

Considering that I hadn't dared to leave the
room in case Amanda was lying in wait for
me, and that I'd only been able to get a little
of the make-up off with tissues, it seemed

kind of funny that I should have picked the beauty contest card.

'They sure have strange ideas of what's *beautiful* in this game,' Fern said.

'Guys?' Pippa moaned from inside the closet. 'Let me out now, huh?'

'What are the magic words?' I called.

'I won't have any more ideas,' Pippa said. She hammered on the closet door. 'Let me out, guys. I won't have another idea for the rest of my life. Really! I promise!'

I looked at the others. 'Do you think she's learned her lesson?' I asked them.

'How long has she been in there?' Cindy asked.

'A quarter of an hour,' I said. I raised my voice so that Pippa would be able to hear. 'I was thinking of leaving her in there overnight.'

'I think you should let her out,' Cindy said.

I crawled over to the closet, pulled back the catch and opened the door. Pippa peered blearily out at me from under my hanging clothes.

'So I guess you don't want to hear my idea?' she said.

'No,' I said. 'I don't!'

Pippa came crawling out of the closet. She handed me a sock and stretched her arms and

56

legs. 'Not even if it's the most brilliant idea in the entire history of the human race?'

'Not even if it's the most brilliant idea in the entire history of the human race *and* Pippa Kane,' I said.

'OK,' Pippa said. 'I know when to keep my mouth shut.' She looked over at the Monopoly board. 'Can I play?'

'We're in the middle of a game,' Cindy said. 'You can be banker. I don't trust Fern.'

'Excuse me!' Fern said. 'What exactly does that mean?'

'It means putting you in charge of the money is like putting Dracula in charge of a blood bank,' Cindy said. 'You cheat!'

'I do not cheat,' Fern said. 'I improvise.'

'Keep it cool, guys,' I said. 'I can go and visit Amanda if I want an argument.'

We played until it was time for them to head home. Amanda had gone out somewhere so I was safe from her for the time being.

After saying goodbye to my friends, I went up to the bathroom and scraped all the gunk off my face. Pippa had taken that awful wig with her. I sure didn't want to see *that* again. I put Amanda's clothes back in the wash and went back to my room.

I felt I needed to cheer myself up, so I got Craig's letters out and re-read them. You know, I could have *kicked* myself for telling him I was twelve and sending him that picture of Amanda! If I'd only told the truth I could have been looking forward to actually meeting him in a few days. As it was, I was using up every ounce of my energy trying to come up with a way of keeping him as far from Four Corners as I could.

After I'd finished reading through all of Craig's letters, I thought I'd better put away the Monopoly board. I was just collecting all the Monopoly money together and sorting it out, when I spotted a small sheet of paper with Pippa's handwriting on it.

I hadn't noticed her writing anything, but then the game had gotten kind of hectic towards the end. It always does when we play with Fern. She really gets carried away. Like you'll discover five-hundred dollar bills that she shouldn't have suddenly appearing in her hand out of nowhere.

Pippa's note:

*'I know you're not interested, but I'm going to tell you my idea anyway. I think you should ask Amanda to impersonate you for the afternoon when Craig comes over. Craig won't realize she's not you, and everything will be just fine.'*

I stared at Pippa's note.

Amanda? *Impersonate* me?

Well done, Pippa – that was your craziest one yet.

Hmmm. Wait a minute.

On the other hand, maybe it was just stupid enough to work.

It was a shame, though, that Pippa hadn't given me a clue how to convince Amanda to help me out. Now *that* would have been some idea!

# Chapter Seven

'Stacy,' Mom said. 'Come here a minute, will you?'

It was later that same day. I'd gone down to the kitchen for a snack. Mom was sitting at the table reading some papers. She glanced up as I came in and I saw her do a double-take as she got a look at my face.

'Just a minute,' I said, shoving my head in the fridge.

'Right now, young lady,' Mom said.

I walked over to the table. I let my head hang, hoping my hair would cover my face.

Mom put her hand under my chin and lifted my head.

'What have you been doing?' she said.

I'd managed to scrape nearly all the make-up off. I nearly removed my skin in the process! I was in the bathroom for half an hour. But there were still a few smears left, and Mom's eagle-eyes had spotted them.

'We were just doing makeovers on each

other,' I said. I sat down with my chin in my hands. 'Pippa and Cindy were trying to make me look pretty,' I said gloomily. I wrinkled my forehead and looked at Mom. 'It didn't work.'

Mom stroked my hair. 'You already *are* pretty,' she said.

'How can I be pretty?' I said. I bared my braces in a big false grin. 'I'm a metalmouthed freak. There isn't one boy in the whole wide world who'd think I was pretty! And I've got these dumb freckles. And my hair is boring. And I'm skinny.'

'Wow!' Mom said. 'Someone's feeling sorry for herself.' Her eyes suddenly lit up. 'I know what this is all about. It's because Craig is coming to visit, isn't it?'

'No.'

'Get out of here!'

I looked at Mom. All of a sudden I really wanted to tell her everything.

But I already *knew* what Mom would say. She'd say I should come clean with Craig. She'd say I should call him and tell him that I'm really ten years old and that the photo I sent was of my older sister, Amanda. She'd say I should tell him that I pretended to be twelve because I was worried he might not want to write to me anymore if he knew how young I was.

'OK, it's true,' I said. 'I guess I am a little nervous about meeting him.' I looked at Mom. 'Wouldn't you be?'

'Uh-huh,' Mom said with a nod. 'But that's part of the fun. Butterflies in the stomach. Wondering if he'll like you. And wondering if you'll like him. And I'll let you in on a little secret, Stacy. In Pennsylvania there's a boy right now with exactly the same butterflies in his stomach.' She leaned over and gave me a hug. 'Why don't you call him and make the arrangements?'

I looked at the wall clock.

'It's a little late,' I said. 'I'll call him tomorrow.'

'Do that,' Mom said. 'And, hey, you're pretty, right?'

I nodded.

A car engine sounded real close outside the house.

'Dad!' I said.

I went to the front door to meet Dad. He gave me a big *hello* hug like he always does.

'Hello, sweetheart!' he said. 'And how's my little girl?'

'Dad? Am I pretty?' I asked.

'Are you kidding me?' he said. 'Of course you are!'

I took Dad's hand, hauling him along the hall and into the kitchen.

'I don't get it,' I said. 'Amanda's pretty, right?'

'Yup,' Dad said, as Mom came over for a hello kiss.

'But I don't look anything like Amanda,' I said. 'So how can we both be pretty?'

Mom looked at Dad. 'She's panicking about her pen pal, Craig, coming here to visit,' she said.

'Oh, right,' Dad said. He sat down and dragged me up into his lap. 'It's perfectly simple,' he said. 'Amanda is pretty like an Amanda ought to be. And you're pretty like a Stacy ought to be. Both totally different and both the prettiest pair of girls in the world.'

I wish that was true!

Oh, what the heck. I can't spend my whole life with my head in a bag because I don't look like my *sister*! And, anyway, I've got other problems to think about.

*  *  *

I knocked on Amanda's door.

'Enter!' she called from inside.

Enter???? Can you believe that *anyone* would actually say that? Only Amanda!

I opened the door. Amanda was lying on her bed reading a magazine.

'What do you want?' she asked in this really icy voice.

'I came to apologize about earlier,' I said. 'And I wanted to explain.'

She gave a sort of royal wave of her hand. 'You don't have to do that,' she said. 'You can't help being weird.'

'Are you going to let me speak?' I asked. I could think of plenty of things to say back to her, but I didn't want this to turn into an argument.

'It's a free country,' Amanda said.

'OK,' I said. 'I admit that we were trying to make me up to look like you. But it wasn't the way you think. We weren't doing it as a joke.'

I went and sat at the end of Amanda's bed.

'So?' she said. 'What *were* you doing?'

I looked at her. 'Promise you won't laugh?'

'Huh?'

'I mean it, Amanda,' I said. 'You've got to promise not to laugh.'

'OK,' Amanda said. 'I promise.'

I took a deep breath. Boy, was this going to be embarrassing!

\* \* \*

'You promised not to laugh!' I yelled as I

swiped at Amanda with a pillow. 'You promised!'

Amanda was rolling on the floor, curled up and clutching her sides. And *shrieking* with laughter.

She was laughing so much that I'm surprised she didn't have an *accident*!

I swiped and whacked and walloped her with the pillow.

'It's not *that* funny!' I hollered. 'It's not funny at all!'

Amanda sat up, wiping her eyes.

I knelt on the bed, glaring down at her.

'Are you finished laughing at me?' I asked.

She nodded, but her shoulders were still shaking.

'OK,' I said. 'So now I'm supposed to call Craig and make plans for him to come and visit. I don't know what to *do*, Amanda! Stop that!'

She was still shaking, like a volcano about to erupt.

'I – ' She opened her mouth, but she only got one word out before she collapsed into a fit of giggles again.

'Oh, forget it!' I shouted. 'I never should have told you!'

I jumped off the bed and headed for the door.

I didn't slam the door behind me. Slamming doors is really childish. I closed the door real quietly and walked to my room. I shut my own door quietly behind me. No slamming doors. No stamping feet. No yelling or screaming.

I was determined about one thing. I was going to deal with this little problem in an entirely calm, sophisticated and *adult* way.

If only I knew what that was.

# Chapter Eight

I met up with the guys outside my locker at school the next morning.

I thanked Pippa for her helpful suggestion, and explained how I had decided to tell Amanda the whole thing in the hope that she might want to help me out.

'And what did she say?' Pippa asked. 'Is she going to help?'

'Let me put it this way, Pippa,' I said. 'She laughed so hard that I thought she was going into cardiac arrest.'

'But what about after she'd finished laughing?' Cindy asked.

'What do you mean, *after*?' I said. 'She hasn't *stopped* yet!'

'So what *are* you going to do?' Fern asked.

'What choice do I have?' I said. 'I'm going to have to call Craig and tell him the truth. And then I guess I'll have to find myself another pen pal.'

* * *

To tell the truth, Amanda hadn't actually laughed out loud that morning at breakfast. But every now and then she'd look at me and I could see her shoulders shaking as if she was having real trouble keeping all the laughter bottled up.

Now that I'd decided I was going to tell Craig the truth, I wanted to make sure Amanda didn't blurt anything to Mom. It wasn't that I didn't want Mom to know, but I wanted to tell her *myself*. The last thing I needed right then was for Amanda to spill the whole humiliating story as if it was the joke of the century.

Which is why, at lunchtime that day, I went looking for Amanda. I wanted to make sure she didn't say anything to anyone at home until I'd had the chance to sort it all out my own way.

Amanda took some finding. In the end I headed for the girls room, which is where she sometimes hangs out with her Bimbo friends, talking about Bimbo things and fixing their hair and stuff like that.

She wasn't there, but I needed to use the girls room anyway. I was all done and about to let myself out of the stall when I heard the door open and I heard Cheryl Ruddick give one of her hyena-like yells of laughter.

Cheryl Ruddick! A name to send shivers down the spine of any halfway normal person. She was Amanda's best friend, and possibly my *worst* enemy.

Did I tell you that my mom writes rhymes for greetings cards? Well, poetry must run in the family, because I wrote a poem all about Cheryl:

*Cheryl Ruddick looks like a hyena*
*Except she's a whole lot meaner*
*She's stuck-up and sarcastic*
*And her hair looks like plastic*
*You'd know what I mean if you'd seen her.*

And it's all true, except the part about her hair looking like plastic. It looks more like she borrowed it from a down-and-out porcupine, but I had to find a rhyme for 'sarcastic'. Poets are allowed to do that, Mom says. It's called poetic licence. (I guess that means you can get away with stuff as long as it rhymes.)

I kept really quiet and listened.

There was someone else laughing out there, too.

'Oh, wow!' Cheryl yelled, 'That's *priceless*! Is that kid sister of yours dumb or what?'

'I haven't told you the best part yet!' That was Amanda's voice. They were laughing about *me*! Amanda must have been telling them all about me and the picture and *everything*!

'You mean it gets better?'

Arrgh! That was Rachel Goldstein's voice. Rachel Goldstein is the final proof that human beings evolved from apes. Except she hasn't evolved quite so far as the rest of us. She looks like a gibbon. A gibbon with carrot-coloured hair.

So, *she* was out there as well. For heaven's sake, how big an audience had Amanda brought in here? The entire eighth grade?

'You bet,' Amanda said. 'Because the latest is that this Craig kid is coming over to visit.'

'I *love* it! Your kid sister is such a nerd, Amanda!' I recognized Natalie Smith's squeaky voice.

Natalie is totally vain. She's got this long ash-blonde hair right down to her backside. From behind she does look pretty amazing. But from in front she looks like a startled gopher. And she's got this eenie-weenie squeaky little voice.

So all four members of the Bimbo Brigade were out there.

Was I mad! I went crashing out with steam coming out of my ears! I hadn't been that mad at Amanda for as long as I could remember.

The laughter stopped as though someone had thrown a switch.

I ignored the others. I marched straight up to Amanda.

'Hi, Stacy . . .' she began, looking really guilty. 'We were just – '

'I know what you were just doing!' I said. 'I just want you to know that I'm never going to forgive you for this. I'll hate you forever and I'm never going to speak to you again!'

That was it. That was all I had to say. I turned around, and without looking left or right, I marched straight out of there in total silence.

Now, come on, was that impressive or what?

I've got to admit I was shaking a little as I walked down the hall. My legs felt a little wobbly, but at least I hadn't just burst into tears back there, although that's what I'd felt like doing.

I heard the sound of the girls room door opening, and someone came running up behind me.

'Hey, Stacy?' It was Amanda.

I kept on walking. I didn't even look at her.

She ran to catch up with me again. 'Look,' she said, 'I know you're upset, but I'm sorry. I'm really, really sorry.'

Ignore!

'Stacy?' She grabbed hold of my arm. 'It was a really rotten thing to do,' she said. 'I'm sorry, I'm sorry, I'm sorry. What else can I say? Stacy? Will you *look* at me?'

I stopped and stared at her.

'That's better,' she said with a hopeful kind of smile. 'You don't really hate me, do you?'

'Give me one good reason why I shouldn't,' I said frostily.

Amanda frowned. 'Well, because you're far too intelligent a person to waste all that energy in *hating* someone when they're really, really, really sorry for what they did.'

'Nice try,' I said. 'But no sale!' I glared at her. 'I told you about Craig in confidence. And what's the first thing you do? You come running into school to tell all your Bimbo friends.'

'I'll make up for it,' Amanda said. 'I'll do anything you say. You can't be mad at me for long, Stacy. You know you can't.'

'Yeah, right,' I said. 'Well, why don't you just hold your breath until I stop being mad at you, Amanda?'

'OK,' Amanda said. 'I'm going to hold my breath until you forgive me!' She took a big gulp of air.

I stared up at her. I folded my arms and waited. The first thing I noticed was that her cheeks started to go pink after about half a minute. Then her forehead wrinkled and her eyes started to look like they were about to pop out. Then she sucked her cheeks in and made her lips go into a penguin face.

Then she went cross-eyed. Her face was bright red by now. I could feel myself starting to weaken.

'Breathe, you big dummy!' I said.

Amanda shook her head and made a cutting motion of her finger across her throat.

No one can *really* hold their breath until they pass out, can they?

Amanda started to stagger around the hallway, clutching at her throat with both hands. Her face looked like it was about to go pop!

Then she came crashing down on her knees in front of me. She clasped her hands together in a pleading gesture.

That was it. That did it. I couldn't help myself anymore. I just started laughing.

'I forgive you!' I said.

'Blaaaaggghhhhhh!!!!!' Amanda's breath exploded out and she did a sort of theatrical collapse on the floor.

She lay on her back, grinning up at me. 'Do you really forgive me?' she panted.

'I don't know,' I said. 'Maybe. Why were you making fun of me back there?' I asked.

Amanda clambered to her feet. 'You weren't supposed to *know*,' she said.

'That's not the point,' I said.

'Oh, come on, Stacy,' Amanda said. 'How often do you and your little buddies sit around laughing at me? I bet you do it all the time.'

'We do not,' I said. I smiled. 'Not *all* the time.' I looked at her. 'Did you mean it?'

'Did I mean what?' Amanda asked.

'What you said just now, about doing *anything* to prove you're sorry.'

'No,' Amanda said. 'I lied.'

'Oh! Right! Well you can just go and – '

'Wait! Wait!' Amanda interrupted with a laugh. 'I was kidding. What do you want me to do?'

I heard voices at the end of the hall. The rest of the Bimbos had come out of the girls room and were heading towards us.

'There's no time to tell you now,' I said. 'I'll explain after school, OK?'

'I'm not doing anything stupid,' Amanda said.

'Don't worry,' I told her. 'All you have to do is a little acting.'

I left her looking kind of baffled.

*Don't sweat it, Amanda. All will be revealed.*

# Chapter Nine

'Now let me get this straight,' Amanda said. 'You want me to pretend to be *you* for an afternoon with Craig?'

'You got it,' I said. 'It's as simple as that. Nothing to it.'

We were in my bedroom after school that day and I had just explained my idea to Amanda. (OK, *Pippa's* idea. Excuse me, but I'm trying to *forget* that Pippa thought of it. That way I was hoping there was some chance of it actually *working*.)

'It'll never work,' Amanda said.

'Sure it will,' I said.

'Stacy, read my lips: It'll never work. It's crazy. It's from Loonieville!' She stared at me. 'It's the kind of stupid scheme your friend Pippa would come up with.'

I gave her a long, slow look. 'I can see you're not completely convinced about this,' I said. 'Let me go through it again for you.'

'Don't bother,' Amanda said. 'For a start, Mom and Dad would never go along with it.'

'I wasn't planning to bring them in on it,' I said.

'What are you going to do, then?' Amanda asked. 'Give them a few dollars and send them to the movies for the afternoon, Stacy? Get real! They're going to be in the house. They'll notice Craig calling me Stacy. Believe me, they'll get suspicious.'

'Yeah, but only if I meet Craig *here*,' I said. 'Not if we arrange to meet someplace else.'

Amanda thought about this for a minute. 'OK,' she said, 'let's suppose you fix it so Mom and Dad don't get to meet Craig. Let's say he agrees to meet you near the train station. The minute I open my mouth he'll know I'm not you. We don't sound the *same*, Stacy.'

'But he doesn't know *what* I sound like,' I said. 'And if you call him tonight to make the arrangements, he *will* think you sound like me.'

'You want me to call him tonight?' Amanda said.

'Why wait?' I said. 'Strike while the iron is hot.'

'What iron?'

'Huh?'

'What *iron*?' Amanda asked. There are times when Amanda picks up on the weirdest things.

'How should I know what iron?' I said. 'The kind of iron you press clothes with, I guess. Does it matter?'

'But why *strike*?' Amanda asked. 'Strike means *hit*. You don't *hit* clothes when you iron them. You just press down on them.'

'Will you keep to the point, please?' I said. 'I want you to call Craig tonight and make arrangements for me – *you*, I mean – to meet up with him at that diner by the train station. You know the one I mean?'

'Casey's?' Amanda said.

'That's the one,' I said. 'Then you keep him busy for the afternoon – pretending to be me, of course. Then he gets back on the train, goes back home, and everyone is happy. Craig and I keep writing to each other and he'll never know the difference.'

Amanda grinned. 'And he'll be able to keep telling his friends that he's got this really, totally, utterly, breathtakingly gorgeous pen pal.'

Sigh! Talk about conceited! Maybe I would have been better off telling Craig the truth.

'Maybe Craig has got some hunky older friends that might want to write me,' Amanda said, gazing into the distance with a dreamy look in her eyes. 'Show me that picture of him again.'

I handed over the photo. 'They'll want to write to *me*,' I pointed out. 'Not *you*.'

She looked at the photo and shook her head. 'No,' she said. 'He's too young for me. But he's kind of cute, I guess. He doesn't have an older brother, does he?'

'Yes, he does,' I said. 'But *he* isn't coming.'

'Oh, too bad,' Amanda said.

'Can we get back to the point?' I asked. 'Are you going to do it for me?'

'I guess it could be fun,' Amanda said. 'I always kind of liked the idea of being an actor.'

'I thought you wanted to be an artist,' I said.

'I can be both.' Amanda struck a theatrical pose. 'By day she was an artist, working in her California beach-house studio,' she said breathlessly. 'But by night, in the restaurants and clubs of Beverly Hills, she became Amanda l'Amour, star of the silver screen. Courted by the richest and most powerful men in Hollywood, she – '

I curled my hands into a cone around my mouth. 'Earth calling Amanda,' I announced. 'Earth calling Amanda! Come in, please! Your brain has been repaired and is waiting to be picked up.'

She looked at me. 'What?' she said.

'Does this mean you'll do it?' I asked.

'I guess,' Amanda said with a toss of her hair. 'I mean, how difficult can it be to act like *you.*'

'What's that supposed to mean?' I said.

She clasped her hands together between her knees and put on this simpering kind of voice. 'And my very best friend of all is my cat Benjamin. He's just so cute. But then I love *all* animals. I've got a tiger poster on the wall above my bed and I have a wildlife magazine sent to me every month.'

'I don't sound anything like that!' I said. 'Anyway, Craig likes animals, too. He likes stuff to do with animals and he's interested in astronomy, too.'

'Really?' Amanda said. 'Astronomy, huh? At least we'll have something to talk about.'

'Huh?' I said. 'Since when have you been interested in astronomy?'

'For always,' Amanda said. 'I've always been interested in it.'

She *had*? Well, that was the first I'd heard of it.

'Do you want me to call now?' she asked.

I suddenly felt nervous. What if it all went wrong? What if Craig realized it wasn't me? Panic!

Amanda took Craig's latest letter out of my hand and got up off my bed.

'I'll use the phone in Mom and Dad's room,' Amanda said. 'We don't want Mom accidentally hearing the arrangements.'

I followed Amanda down the hall and into Mom and Dad's bedroom. She sat on the edge of the bed and picked up the receiver.

'Don't say anything dumb,' I said anxiously. 'Just make the arrangements and hang up. OK?'

'I've got to be friendly,' Amanda said as she pressed out Craig's number.

'Yeah, but he'll be expecting *my* kind of friendly, not *your* kind of friendly,' I said.

'What are you talking about?' Amanda said. 'I know how to behave on the phone. If you think I'm some kind of total idiot then you shouldn't have – oh! Hi! is Craig Newman there?' she said into the receiver. 'Oh, great! Yes. Tell him it's Amand – *oh*! Uh, ha, ha, no! Could you tell him it's Stacy, please. That's me. Stacy Allen! It's *Stacy* Allen for him. Thank you.'

Amanda put her hand over the receiver. 'Phew! Nice save, huh? Stacy? Why are you crawling under the bed?'

'Because I can't bear to listen!' I said from my hiding place. I squirmed around and stuck my head out. 'Just hang up, Amanda, please. I'll write and tell him I've been kidnapped by aliens.'

'Oh, calm down,' Amanda said. 'It'll be fine.'

'Pippa!' I whispered under my breath. 'You wait 'til I get my hands on you!'

'Hi!' Amanda said. 'Craig? Yeah, it's me. Yeah, great. Uh – huh? Yeah. Right!' She laughed.

That was hopeless. I wanted to be able to hear what Craig was saying. I came out from under the bed and put my head right up close to the receiver. I tweaked Amanda's wrist so the earpiece turned and I was able to listen in.

I heard: ' . . . is that OK?' He had a nice voice. I liked his voice right away. But I'd missed the first part of what he'd been saying. Was what OK?

'Sure,' Amanda said. 'No problem. No problem at all.'

I poked her. 'What's no problem?' I mouthed silently.

'Just a second, Craig,' Amanda said. 'Someone's trying to talk to me.' She put her hand over the mouthpiece. 'For heaven's sake, *what*?'

'What's no problem?' I whispered.

'I'll tell you in a minute,' Amanda said. 'Just shut *up*!' She took her hand away from the mouthpiece. 'Craig? Hi. Sorry about that. My pesky little sister wants to use the phone after me.'

'Oh, right, is that your sister, Amanda?' I heard Craig say. 'The one you told me about?'

'Say yes,' I whispered.

'Yes,' Amanda said into the receiver. She put her hand over the mouthpiece.

'What have you been telling him about me?' she asked.

'Nothing,' I said. 'Honest. Hardly anything.'

That wasn't really true, but it didn't seem like a good time to confess what I'd actually told Craig about my kid sister, Amanda. I'd kind of given him the impression that she was a little dumb. I thought, if I was pretending to be Amanda, why not give myself a kid sister? A kind of swap, see?

'Are you still there?' I heard Craig say.

'Yes. I'm here,' Amanda said into the phone. 'Hey, Craig, do you have any brothers or sisters?'

'One older brother,' Craig said.

'Really?' Amanda said. 'How old is he?'

'He's eighteen.'

'Eighteen, huh?' Amanda said. 'Does he have a car?'

I poked her again and gave her a really ferocious glare.

'Yes,' Craig said. 'But he's at college right now. Hey, have you read that article on the Everglades in this month's magazine?'

'Uh . . .' Amanda gave me a look like she didn't know what he was talking about. He meant the wildlife magazine we both subscribe to. I nodded at her. 'Oh,' she said. 'Sure. The Everglades. Yeah, I read the whole thing. It was really interesting.'

'Isn't it amazing that people are draining away all the water?' Craig said.

'Yeah,' Amanda said before I could stop her. 'It's about time someone did something about all that water down there.'

She saw me shaking my head and going: *No!*

Craig laughed. 'Right,' he said. 'Nice joke.'

I put my hand over the mouthpiece.

'It's *supposed* to be wet,' I whispered. 'Losing the water is really bad news.'

'Uh, Craig,' Amanda said, 'look, I'd really like to talk with you some more, but Amanda is bugging me to get off the phone. Can we just make the arrangements for getting together?'

'Sure,' Craig said. 'Why don't you tell me how to get to your house?'

'No,' Amanda said quickly. 'Since you're

coming by train, I thought I could meet you at the station. It'd take you forever to find my house. It's miles away from the station. There's no point wasting half the afternoon getting here. I thought we could maybe have something to eat in a diner. There's a good one right near the station.'

'Sure,' Craig said. 'That sounds great. The train I'll be on gets to Four Corners at noon.'

'Great,' Amanda said. 'I'll be there to meet you. Look, I've got to go; my sister is being a real *pain*.'

'OK,' I heard Craig say. 'I'll see you there. I'm really looking forward to it.'

'Me too,' Amanda said. 'Hey, by the way, I'm a Taurus!'

'Sorry?' Craig said. 'You're *what*?'

'Taurus,' Amanda said. 'The bull. What are you?'

'I . . . uh . . .'

'We can talk about it when we see each other,' Amanda said. 'I have to go now. Nice talking to you. 'Bye-ee.'

She put the phone down.

'Well,' she said. 'That went OK, didn't it? No problems.'

I was feeling a little shell-shocked by it all. 'Why did you say that about you being a

*Taurus*?' I asked. 'What did you tell him that for?'

'You told me he was interested in astronomy,' Amanda said. She grinned. 'I was just letting him know that I know one or two things about the subject.'

'That's astroLOGY, you idiot, not *astronomy*! Astronomy is all about *real* stuff. It's a science. It's about stars and planets and what they all do out there.'

'Really?' Amanda said. 'Are you sure about that?'

'Trust me,' I groaned, putting my head in my hands. Suddenly I felt very panicky. 'Amanda, this isn't going to work.'

'For goodness' sake, have a little *faith* in me,' Amanda said. 'It'll be fine.'

'It won't, it won't!' I moaned. 'He'll know you're not me the moment you open your mouth. You think the Everglades need draining out! You think astronomy is all about horoscopes! I'm going to have to call back and tell him the truth.'

'Don't you dare,' Amanda said. 'I'm looking forward to this. It'll be fun. I kind of like the idea of pretending to be someone else. Even if it *is* only you.' She looked at me. 'Hey, don't look so worried. He didn't suspect anything, did he?'

'I guess I could give you a crash course in wildlife and stuff,' I said. 'Just so you'd know *something*. We've got nearly a week and a half before he's coming.'

'Oh, yeah,' Amanda said. 'That thing you were asking about, remember? Right at the beginning?'

'I remember,' I said suspiciously. 'So what exactly did you say was OK?'

Amanda gave me a big grin. 'His folks have changed the date for their visit to Indianapolis,' she said cheerfully. 'They've brought it forward a week. He's coming *this* weekend.'

Erk! Waaaauugh! Thud!

That was me *fainting* right there on the carpet.

Well? What *else* was there to do?

# Chapter Ten

'*This* weekend?' Cindy said. 'He's coming this weekend?'

'That's right,' I said.

'Today's Friday,' Pippa said.

'It sure is,' I said.

'And tomorrow is Saturday,' Pippa pointed out.

'Give the girl a prize,' I said. 'She knows what order the days of the week come in.'

Fern grinned. 'You're very calm about this, Stacy,' she said.

I looked at her.

'It's a funny thing,' I said, 'but once you know the *worst* is going to happen, you kind of stop worrying.' I shrugged. 'What can I do? Craig has spoken to Amanda on the phone. Amanda thinks it's going to be a real blast to spend tomorrow afternoon pretending to be me. Craig is going to think my brain is on vacation.' I opened this month's wildlife magazine. 'And I'm going to look for a new pen pal.'

Let me explain how I came to be this calm. After all, I'd been in a state of total panic the night before.

My mom helped. You see, when my mom gets stressed out she has this routine to calm herself. Sometimes Mom will get stressed out with her work. Sometimes she gets stressed because Sam has eaten an important telephone number that she'd forgotten to move out of his reach. Sometimes she gets stressed because Amanda won't do her homework.

You may not believe this, but now and then, Mom even gets a little stressed by things that *I* do.

Anyway, when she's on the verge of totally freaking out, she goes and sits cross-legged on her bed with her eyes closed and thinks of a calm, blue ocean.

And according to Mom, half an hour of thinking of a calm blue ocean nearly always does the trick.

So, after the Nightmare Phone Call, I went to my room, sat cross-legged on my bed, and thought of a calm blue ocean.

Except that these little boats kept sailing across my calm blue ocean. Amanda was sitting in one of the boats.

'Hi,' she kept saying. 'My name is Stacy Allen. I like astronomy. I'm a Taurus. What are you?'

And another boat had Pippa in it.

'I've had a really good idea,' Pippa was saying. 'Why don't we make a papier-maché puppet of Amanda. You could work it with strings through a hole in the ceiling. Craig would never notice the difference.'

Fern was in another.

'Hey, Stacy, I've been speaking to some friends of mine in the Martian FBI. They say they can fix you with a whole new identity. Here, they've made up this passport for you in the name of Stacy *Alien*. You'll be able to just *disappear*.'

And Cindy, of course.

'I think the answer is a slice of lemon meringue pie. What do you say, Benjamin?'

Which is when I noticed Cindy was wearing Benjamin as a hat. Which was also when I noticed that my calm blue ocean had changed into blue Jell-o.

'Stacy, wake up, honey; it's time to get ready for bed.'

Mom laughed and I woke up.

I'd fallen asleep right out there in the middle of my calm blue ocean. Dumb ocean!

But by the next morning I'd kind of resigned

myself to my fate. Which was why I seemed so calm to my friends that morning in class.

'Aren't you even the least bit worried about the kind of things Amanda is going to say to Craig while she's pretending to be you?' Cindy asked.

'What can I do?' I said.

'There must be *something* you could do,' Pippa said. 'You can't just give up like this.'

'Can't I?' I said. 'Just watch me.'

'Stacy!' Cindy said. 'Snap out of it! You've got to *do* something.'

'Like what?' I said. 'Blow up the train tracks between here and Indianapolis?'

'At least talk to Amanda about it,' Pippa said. 'Make sure she doesn't say anything stupid. Lend her some of your wildlife books. They're only having lunch together. She only needs to be able to say a couple of halfway intelligent things.'

'That'll be halfway too much for her,' I said. 'There's no point in trying to *do* anything, Pippa. I'm *doomed*!'

'You sure are if you do nothing,' Fern said. She shrugged. 'I never thought of you as a quitter, Stacy.'

I glared at her. 'I'm not a quitter!' I said.

'If you say so,' Fern said. 'But it sure looks like it from where I'm standing. Huh, guys?'

90

Pippa and Cindy looked at her, then looked at me. I could see what they were thinking. They agreed with Fern.

'OK,' I said. 'OK! You three just wait! At lunchtime, I'm going to go find Amanda, and I'm going to beat some intelligence into her head, if I have to use an iron bar!'

And do you know something, for a few minutes there, I really believed myself.

\* \* \*

'Stacy, will you leave me *alone*,' Amanda said irritatedly. She was walking with Cheryl. I was tugging at her sleeve and she was doing her best to shake me off like I was some kind of mosquito.

'But we need to talk!' I said.

'Not *now*!' she said. 'I've got things to do.'

'But he's going to be in town in just over twenty-four hours!' I said, pulling at her sleeve. 'You've got to let me tell you some stuff about the things he's interested in.'

Amanda stopped in her tracks and gave me this really maddening pat on the head.

'I think you can leave me to know what *boys* like to talk about,' she said.

'What's the problem?' Cheryl asked.

Amanda smirked at her. 'It's Stacy's boy-friend trouble. I've agreed to help her out.'

'Hee-haww! Hee-haww!' Cheryl let out this big bray of laughter. 'Are you crazy?' she howled. 'Can you imagine how boring that kid is going to be? A boy who likes to write to *Stacy*? Like, nerd to nerd?'

'Why don't you go lie on the highway?' I said to Cheryl. I gave Amanda a pleading look. 'Craig doesn't like the kind of stuff you know about,' I said. 'At least let me lend you a couple of magazines.'

Amanda put her hands on her hips. 'You'd think I was a total dummy from the sound of it!' she said. 'For your information, Miss Stacy Know-it-all, I know lots about a whole load of things. Don't I, Cheryl?'

'Sure,' Cheryl said. '*Interesting* things.' She grinned at me. 'You know what the word *interesting* means, don't you, Stacy? It means not *nerd* stuff.'

I ignored her.

'Then what's the difference between Indian and African elephants?' I asked Amanda.

Amanda just stared at me. 'Huh?'

'It's an easy question,' I said. 'You think you know everything about *everything*. So what's the difference between an Indian and an African elephant?'

'About three thousand miles, I guess,' Amanda said.

'You see!' I yelled. 'You don't know *anything* about stuff like that at *all*.'

'Quit shouting,' Amanda said. 'They've got different size ears. Right?'

'Oh!' I stared at her. 'Right. How did you know that?'

Amanda wagged her finger in front of my eyes. 'You see, Stacy? I'm not as dumb as you think. Just because I don't always have my nose in a book doesn't mean I'm a total bozo.'

I felt a little foolish. I hadn't expected Amanda to know the answer to my elephant question.

I started to wonder. Maybe Amanda knows lots of things, but never bothers talking about them. Wouldn't that be weird? All these years of pretending she was a total airhead, while all along she was stuffed full of information.

'OK,' I said. 'I'm sorry.'

'So I don't want to hear any more about it, OK?' Amanda said.

'I guess not,' I said.

Amanda tossed her hair and the two of them went walking down the hall.

Boy, I guess that put me in my place!

'Hey,' I heard Cheryl say just as they were going around a corner. 'What did you say was different about those elephants?'

'It's easy,' Amanda said as they walked out

of sight. 'We learned it last year. Indian elephants have got these great big ears, and African elephants' ears are really small.'

Oh no! I couldn't believe it! She'd gotten it all wrong! It's *African* elephants that have the big ears!

And it's the golden crested, empty-headed Giant Amanda of America that has the smallest brain of any living creature on earth.

And the next day she was going to meet up with my pen pal Craig, and pretend to be me.

Life gets kind of depressing at times, don't you think?

# Chapter Eleven

Dear Craig,
I am really sorry I wasn't able to meet you on Saturday. I couldn't get out of the house because there was a rogue African elephant blocking our front driveway. Sadly, my little sister, Amanda, whom you will remember I've mentioned in my letters, was squashed to an unrecognizable mush by the elephant on her way back from cheerleading practice. We will all miss her a lot, I think.
                    Yours truly,
                        Stacy

I slipped the letter under the desk to Cindy.

'Stacy!' Ms Fenwick snapped like a crocodile. 'What is *that*?'

'Nothing, ma'am,' I said.

Ms Fenwick came swooping up.

She held her hand out and Cindy reluctantly handed over my fake letter.

Ms Fenwick read it. Now I might have been wrong, but I was sure I saw this little flicker at the edge of her mouth. Like she was trying not to laugh.

'I admire your imaginative powers, Stacy,' Ms Fenwick said, 'But I would prefer if you kept your mind on the subject in question.' She marched back to the front of the class with my letter in her hand.

'And *now*,' she said, 'I'm sure Stacy would like to tell us everything she knows about the landing of the Pilgrim Fathers.'

Right then, I couldn't have cared less about the Pilgrim Fathers. Or the Pilgrim Mothers! And especially not the Pilgrim *Older Sisters*, if there were any!

★　★　★

Determination! That's what Mom says you need if you're going to succeed. Decide what you want and go for it.

What I wanted was to try and force some knowledge about things Craig might want to talk about into Amanda's head before High Noon on Saturday.

I had already loaned Amanda Craig's letters so that she could kind of get to know him through them. She'd said she was going to read them, but I didn't totally *trust* her to bother. She certainly didn't show much interest in finding out anything about the kind of things Craig likes.

'Have you ever heard of subliminal learning?' Pippa said as we sat at our usual table in the cafeteria.

'No, I haven't,' I said. 'And I don't want to.'

'You might,' Pippa said, 'if you let me explain. It might be just the answer you're looking for.'

'Go on, then,' I sighed. 'What is subnormal learning?'

'*Subliminal*,' Pippa said. 'It's a way of teaching people while they're asleep. You can buy tapes and everything. It's supposed to be really good.'

'I'll sign up for it,' Fern said. 'I like the idea of learning everything while I'm asleep.' She grinned. 'Especially if it'll save me having to come to school every day.'

'I think I've heard of it,' Cindy said. 'Don't you put headphones on and let the tapes run through the night?'

'That's right,' Pippa said. 'People learn all sorts of stuff that way. This voice talks straight into your *brain* all night. And when you wake up, you know tons of stuff you didn't know before.'

'Get out of here,' I said.

'Honest!' Pippa said. 'People learn entire *languages* that way.'

'How do you listen to stuff when you're asleep?' I said. 'I bet you're making this up.'

'She isn't,' Cindy said. 'I've heard about it too.'

'It's totally true,' Pippa said. 'Cross my heart and hope to die covered in honey in a pit of tiger ants.'

'OK,' I said, 'I believe you.' (You've *got* to believe someone who crosses her heart and hopes to die covered in honey in a pit of tiger ants, for heaven's sake!) 'But how does it help *me* right now?'

'That's easy,' Pippa said. 'You find a tape that has all the stuff you want Amanda to know when she meets Craig. You plug her into it tonight. And hey, presto! When she wakes up tomorrow morning she'll be a total expert!'

'And where do I get this tape?' I said. 'Assuming for one *second* that I don't think this is the craziest scheme you've come up with for the last two years!'

Pippa shrugged. 'I don't know. Do I have to think of everything?'

'I don't have time to find a store that sells subminimal learning tapes,' I said.

'Sub*lim*inal,' Pippa said. I guess she was kind of proud of knowing that word.

'The whole idea is that this voice whispers into your ear all night while you're asleep, right?' Fern said.

'Right,' Pippa said.

'So it doesn't actually need to be on a tape, does it?' Fern said. 'I mean, someone could creep into your room in the middle of the night and whisper stuff to you while you were asleep. Wouldn't that work?'

'I guess so,' Pippa said.

Fern grinned. 'There you go,' she said, looking at me. 'You don't need a tape. You could do it in person.'

I munched thoughtfully on my sandwich.

Was it a crazy idea?

*Yes, it sure was.*

Would it work?

*Not in a million, million years!*

Did I have any other ideas?

*Nope.*

I sighed and looked at Pippa.

'OK,' I said. 'Run the whole thing by me one more time.'

★ ★ ★

After school that afternoon I stopped by the library and looked for a book on astronomy. I figured while I was *sublamentably* teaching

Amanda about animals, I might as well drop in a few facts about Craig's other big passion.

There were plenty of books on astronomy. Big, thick books with tiny print and weird maps of the sky that didn't make any sense to me at all. Books with sentences that went on and on and on and on for pages.

Boy, if you weren't asleep already, some of those *sentences* would sure put you to sleep.

But then I found a skinny little book called *A Beginner's Guide to the Night Sky*. Aha! That was more like it. It was written in nice, simple words. The kind of words that even Amanda would understand.

I took the book out and headed home.

The plan was simple. I'd wait until I was sure Amanda was asleep, then I'd creep into her room, park myself on the floor by her pillow and whisper some useful information to her for an hour or so.

I know what you're thinking. You're thinking I must have gone completely crazy. Well, maybe I had, but people weren't exactly forming a long line at my door with any other ideas.

Meanwhile, I planned to spend a few hours making some notes of useful stuff for Amanda to know out of my collection of wildlife magazines, and in reading my *Beginner's Guide to the Night Sky*.

The phone was ringing as I got home.

I closed the front door and I was just reaching for the phone when it stopped.

A few seconds later Mom called up from the basement.

'Is that you, Stacy?'

I ran to the basement door. 'Yes, it's me,' I called down.

'Call for you, honey!' she said.

'Thanks.' I sat on the stairs with the phone in my lap.

'Hello,' I said. I heard the click of Mom's receiver being put down.

'Stacy?' It was a boy's voice.

No it wasn't! It wasn't *a* boy's voice. It wasn't just *any* boy's voice. It was Craig's voice!

I dropped the receiver in shock. It went bouncing down the stairs. Whack! Whack! *Whack*! down to the hall carpet.

Very faintly I could hear Craig's voice.

'Hello? Hello? Stacy? Are you there?'

I crept down the stairs and kneeled in front of the receiver.

'Stacy? It's Craig. Hello? Is there anyone there?'

I gave a little whimper. What do I do? What do I do?

*Come on, Stacy Allen, are you a wimp or what?*
I'm a wimp.

*No you're not! Think of something real quick. Pick that phone up.*

I picked the receiver up.

'Hello?' I said.

'Oh! There you are,' Craig said. 'I think something must be wrong with the line. Is Stacy there, please?'

Darn! Well, that cleared one question up. I obviously didn't sound anything like Amanda on the phone. Craig had known it wasn't Amanda's voice right away.

'She's not in right now,' I said. 'Can she call you back?'

'Not really,' Craig said. 'We're leaving soon. I called to let Stacy know that I told her the wrong time for tomorrow. I had an out of date schedule. My train gets into Four Corners at a quarter to one, not twelve o'clock. Do you think you could tell her?'

'Sure,' I said.

'Are you her sister?' Craig asked.

'Uh-huh,' I said. 'I'm Amanda.'

'Oh, right. Hi, Amanda,' Craig said. 'I guess Stacy has told you about me, huh?'

'Yeah,' I said.

102

'You won't forget to tell her about the train?' Craig said. 'A quarter to one. Have you got that?'

'Got it,' I said. 'The station at a quarter to one tomorrow.'

'That's it,' Craig said. 'OK, thanks Amanda. Nice speaking to you. Bye.'

'Bye.' I put the phone down.

I'd finally spoken to Craig. My legs felt kind of weak and I had butterflies leaping around in my stomach. Maybe I really *was* coming down with a bad cold after all. I sure felt strange.

Phew!!!! I wiped my arm across my forehead. I really didn't need this kind of thing.

'What was all that about?'

I nearly jumped clean out of my underwear.

It was Mom. She was leaning in the basement doorway with Sam fast asleep in her arms.

'Oh! You really startled me,' I said shakily. 'I didn't hear you come upstairs.'

'I thought Craig was coming over next weekend,' Mom said.

'No,' I said. 'It got changed. Sorry, I meant to tell you. He's coming here tomorrow.' It sounded like Mom had only heard the very end of the phone call. I was sure she'd have said something if she'd heard the part where I told Craig I was Amanda.

'Stacy!' Mom frowned at me. 'I wish you'd told me. I'd have made something nice to eat.' She gave me a little frown. 'Oh, well, I guess I'll be able to come up with something. And your dad will be home tomorrow, so he'll be able to take you to the station to pick Craig up.'

'No!' I almost yelled.

Sam made a muffled noise and gave a little kick and a jerk of his arms.

'Shh!' Mom hissed, gently rocking Sam back to sleep in her arms. 'What do you mean, no? You can't expect the poor boy to find his own way over here.'

'He isn't coming here,' I said.

'Huh?' Mom looked puzzled. 'What do you mean?'

'I mean, he isn't coming *here*,' I said. 'I'm going to meet him at the station. We're going to have something to eat at Casey's, and ... and then we're going to ... uh ... do some ... other stuff,' I said.

'I'm not so sure that's a good idea, Stacy,' Mom said. 'I don't like the idea of you going off all by yourself and meeting up with boys I don't know.' She shook her head. 'No, I think it'd be a much better idea for your dad to pick him up and bring him back here for the afternoon.'

'No,' I said desperately. 'I don't *want* him to come back here. And . . . and I won't *be* on my own with him. Amanda is coming with me.'

'Why don't you want him to come here?' Mom said. 'Are you ashamed of us or something?'

'Of course not,' I said. 'It's just that . . . I . . . I . . .' I took a big breath. 'To be honest with you, Mom, I don't really *like* the guy.'

'But you've been writing to him for months, Stacy,' Mom said. 'You're always telling me how much you have in common. I don't get it. What suddenly made you change your mind?'

I shrugged. 'I guess I just don't like his *voice*,' I said. 'Look, Mom, it's no big deal. Amanda and I are going to meet him at the station tomorrow. The three of us will have something to eat, and then we'll maybe go to the mall or take a walk in Maynard Park. Then he'll get back on the train and go home.'

Mom gave me one of her long, slow looks.

She was about to say something when Sam gave a kick and a wriggle and let out a yell.

'I think his diaper needs changing,' I said.

Mom gave me a funny look, and then walked past me up to the bathroom.

Thanks, baby brother, you got me off the hook nicely, there. Temporarily, at least.

# Chapter Twelve

I had time to fill Amanda in on what had happened before Mom got to her.

Dad was going to be home late, and Sam was asleep upstairs. Mom, Amanda and I were sitting at the dinner table.

'Stacy tells me you'll be going with her to meet Craig,' Mom said to Amanda.

'I sure will,' Amanda said. She grinned. 'Don't worry, Mom. I'll make sure he's not a weirdo.'

Mom looked at me. 'What exactly was wrong with his voice?'

'There's nothing wrong with his voice,' Amanda said.

Rats! I'd told her that Mom was on the prowl about Craig not coming to our house, but I'd forgotten to fill her in on the reason I'd given Mom for not wanting him here.

In movies, the thing to do is to give someone who's about to say something dumb a quick kick under the table.

Kick!

'Ow!' I said as my foot bashed against the table leg. How come that never happens in movies?

'What's wrong?' Mom asked.

'I banged my foot against the table leg,' I said, rubbing it.

Mom looked at Amanda. 'Stacy told me she didn't want him here because she didn't like his voice,' Mom said. 'So when did you hear his voice, Amanda?'

'I haven't,' Amanda said.

'You just said there was nothing wrong with his voice,' Mom said to her. 'Why did you say that if you've never heard it?'

'Oh! His *voice*?' Amanda said. 'Sorry, I thought you meant . . . uh . . . I thought . . . Stacy? Could you pass the ketchup, please?'

'Well?' Mom said. 'I'm waiting for someone to start making some sense around here.'

'I had a few words with him over the phone a couple of days ago,' Amanda said. 'Uh . . . Stacy was . . . uh . . . talking to him and she . . . uh . . . came and fetched me to . . . uh . . . check out his voice.'

'That's right,' I interrupted. 'And Amanda agreed with me that there was something strange about his voice. And so we thought it would be a better idea if we met him over at the station rather than bring him back here. Isn't that right, Amanda?'

'Yup,' Amanda said, nodding. 'That's pretty much what happened, OK.'

Mom leaned her chin in her hands and stared at us.

'What?' Amanda and I said at the same time.

'I don't know,' Mom said. 'That's what I'm trying to figure out.'

'There's nothing *to* figure out,' I said.

'Fine,' Mom said, picking up her knife and fork. 'If you don't want to tell me what this is all about, I guess you don't have to.' She shrugged. 'I'm certainly not going to *force* you to tell me if you don't want to.'

She didn't say another word about it for the rest of the meal. But, you know, I could kind of feel her *thinking* about it. And in some ways, that was even worse.

\* \* \*

I spent a while up in my room. I had two things to do. One was to read up on some of that astronomy stuff for later. The other was to be a cat bed for Benjamin.

I lay on my front on the floor, reading the book while Benjamin made himself a comfortable nest in the small of my back.

"The more you look at the night sky, the more you see!" the book began. "For thousands of years humans have turned their eyes to the stars in wonder and awe."

I read up on stars and constellations. I read that some of the things that look like stars are actually planets. I read about how far all the stars were away from each other. I've got to admit, I'd never paid any real attention to that kind of stuff. Sure, I'd looked up at the stars and thought, Wow! But that was about as far as it went.

But now that I was actually reading about it, I could see why Craig found it all so interesting. In some ways I really wished I hadn't let Craig think I was Amanda! I would have really enjoyed talking to Craig about all this stuff I was finding out about.

I would have gone out into the backyard for a look at the sky right then and there if Benjamin hadn't been fast asleep on me. Benjamin isn't the sort of cat who would understand why his bed wanted to go and gawp at the sky in the middle of his nap.

Eventually I had to disturb the Sleeping Prince because it was *my* bedtime.

Dad got home while I was in the bathroom brushing my teeth. He tucked me in and kissed me goodnight. I snuggled under the covers and Benjamin came and dumped himself across my legs. I read for a little while, and then turned my bedside light off. I had to let Mom and Dad think I was asleep.

I watched the bright red numbers slowly click over on my bedside clock. The one thing I couldn't do was fall asleep. I had things to do. I had subluminous teaching to do!

* * *

'Stars,' I whispered. 'Range in size from the small, or Dwarf, through medium, to Red Giant and, the largest stars of all, the Super Giants.'

I carefully shifted my position on the carpet beside Amanda's bed. I'd only been there a couple of minutes and I was already feeling cramped. And you wouldn't believe how awkward it was to kneel there and lean over so my mouth was right up close to her ear. I didn't dare rest my arms on the bed, in case I woke her up. I had the astronomy book open in my lap. I'd shine my pencil flashlight so I could read and remember a couple of sentences, then I'd lean over as far as I could and whisper into Amanda's ear.

Pippa had better be right about this submarine learning stuff! I've got to admit, though, I was feeling like a total idiot!

I shone my flashlight on the open book and read a couple more sentences.

'Stars differ in colour, depending on how hot they are,' I whispered into Amanda's ear. 'The hottest ones are blue and the coolest ones are red.'

I whispered some more information to her about the way the stars move around in the sky, and about how what we see when we look at a star is actually what the star looked like years and years ago because of how long it takes light to travel. (I wasn't sure Amanda would understand all that, but it was written down so I figured I might as well tell her about it.)

'Black holes,' I whispered, 'are formed when Super Giant stars collapse in on themselves. They cannot be seen, but we know they are there because they suck matter into themselves.'

I was about to tell Amanda about *comets* when I got a cramp in my left leg.

'Eeyowww!' I whooped as my calf muscle went *graunch*! I squirmed over and pulled my leg out from under me. I rolled on the carpet, my book flying in one direction and the flashlight rolling off in another as I clutched my leg.

Gradually the clenching pain went away. I

let out a long, relieved breath and opened my eyes. Gee, there's nothing worse than a cramp!

Amanda was leaning over the side of the bed, staring at me in the faint light of my flashlight.

'I just know I'm going to regret asking this,' she said. 'But what the heck are you doing down there, Stacy?'

'I got a cramp,' I said. 'In my leg.'

'You got a cramp?' Amanda said. 'In your leg?'

'That's right. But it's OK, it's gone now.' I sat up. 'Did I wake you up?'

'You?' Amanda said. 'Wake me up? You mean by rolling around on my floor in the middle of the night like some kind of crazy person? No, of course you didn't wake me up, Stacy.' She glared at me. 'What the heck are you *doing* here?'

'I wanted to tell you some stuff about stars,' I said, picking up the book to show her. 'So you'd be able to talk to Craig about it tomorrow.'

Amanda looked at her bedside clock. 'Today, you mean?'

'Oh, yeah. Today. I just wanted to make sure you'd have stuff in common that you could talk about.'

'So you thought you'd come in here in the

middle of the night and wake me up?' Amanda said. 'To talk about stupid, nerdy, useless *stars*? Are you out of your tiny mind, Stacy?'

'I didn't want to wake you up,' I said. 'I only woke you because I got a cramp. You were supposed to, uh . . . look, I know this is going to sound kind of dumb, but – '

'Stacy, I don't want to know,' Amanda said. 'I don't want to hear it.' She turned over and pulled the blankets up over her ears. 'Just get lost,' came her muffled voice from under the covers.

'But Craig – ' I began.

'Go away!' Amanda said.

So much for my attempts at subhuman teaching! I picked up my flashlight and crept to the door. But I wanted to check something out before I went.

'Amanda?' I whispered. 'Just one thing.'

'What!'

'What colour are the hottest stars?'

A pillow came flying through the air towards me. I ducked and tiptoed out into the darkened hallway.

I sneaked back into my room and slid into bed, moving my legs carefully around a large lump that was fast asleep right in the middle. A large cat lump called Benjamin.

I looked at my clock. It was almost a quarter

to one in the morning. In only twelve hours Craig would be hitting town.

*Oh well, look on the bright side, Stacy. In about eighteen hours he'll be gone and it'll all be over.*

One way or another.

# Chapter Thirteen

*Good Morning, Four Corners, Indiana! It's a bright and breezy Saturday morning and the forecast is for clear skies and sunshine all the way! The birds are singing, the cat is meowing for his breakfast and Stacy Allen is hiding under the bed covers. Hey, Stacy! Come on out! There's a train with your name on it, heading this way. This is going to be some kind of* unusual *Saturday.*

You can say *that* again.

I went down for breakfast. Mom was feeding Sam and Dad was reading the morning paper.

Dad looked at me over the top of his paper.

'Your mom says you don't want to bring your friend home,' he said. 'Something to do with his *voice*?'

I really wished I'd thought up a better excuse! The more people *said* it, the dumber it sounded.

'Yeah,' I said. 'He sounded kind of nerdy.'

Dad put his paper down. 'In what way?'

'I don't know,' I said, heading for the toaster. 'In a nerdy kind of way.'

'Do you mean the sound of his voice was nerdy, or that he said nerdy things?' Dad asked.

'There was nothing wrong with his voice that *I* heard when I spoke to him,' Mom said, guiding a spoonful of baby mush into Sam's wide open mouth. 'He sounded like a perfectly nice boy.'

'It was the things he said,' I told them uneasily. 'He said the kind of things that make you think, ew, I wouldn't want *him* to come and visit. Like, like . . .' Brainwave! 'Like Uncle Joss.' Uncle Joss was my mom's older brother. 'You know what you always say about Uncle Joss, Dad,' I said. 'How a visit from him makes you want to move away without leaving a forwarding address.'

'David!' Mom said sharply. (Mom only calls Dad "David" when she's mad at him.) 'What have you been saying about Joss?'

'Nothing,' Dad said, giving me a really annoyed look. 'Maybe I mentioned . . . uh . . . hey, I just remembered. The car needs washing.'

'HMMMM!' Mom growled as Dad slunk out of the kitchen.

I quickly buttered some toast and got out of there, too. I'd created a diversion, but it wouldn't take long for Mom to get back on my case.

She could ask all the questions she liked once Craig was safely out of town again, but just then I didn't want to have to spend any more time explaining what was wrong with Craig's *voice*. Sheesh! I should have said he had fleas or something.

I went upstairs to see how Amanda was doing.

She was still in bed. I gave her a shake.

She mumbled something and tried to squirm deeper under the covers.

'What did you say?' I asked, shaking her.

She woke up suddenly and sat up.

'Wow!' she said. 'That was one weird dream!'

'What were you dreaming about?' I asked her.

'It's too weird,' Amanda said. 'I dreamed that I was in the middle of a cheer when I was suddenly pulled right off my feet and dragged along at super-speed. And all the other cheerleaders were looking at me as I went whooshing past on my backside.'

'Dragged along by what?' I asked. (I'm

always interested in people's dreams. Dreams can be so bizarre!)

'I don't know,' Amanda said, rubbing her eyes. 'Like, by a *magnet*. And I got dragged all the way home, and up the stairs and right into my room. Except that my room was, like, totally black and full of tons of stuff. The couch from the living room. And the washing machine. And Dad's car and a load of kids from school.' She shivered. 'Creepy!'

'You dreamed your room turned into a black hole!' I crowed. 'It *worked*! Subterranean teaching really *works*!'

'What?' Amanda said. 'What the heck are you talking about, Stacy?'

'It doesn't matter,' I said. 'Rats! I wish I'd had time to tell you about more stuff. Hey, Amanda? What colour are the hottest stars?'

Amanda got out of bed. 'How the heck should I know?' she said, pulling her robe on and padding across the floor. 'I didn't even know stars were different colours.'

I followed her into the hall. 'You *do* know,' I told her. 'Think about it!'

'I don't know,' Amanda said as she went into the bathroom.

'You *do*!'

She gave a snort of annoyance. 'Sky-blue-pink!' she said as she slammed the door in my

119

face. 'Now leave me alone and stop asking dumb questions first thing in the morning.'

Sky-blue-pink? If you left out *sky* and *pink* she'd said *blue*! And blue was right! The hottest stars were blue.

Maybe I was clutching at straws?

* * *

'If he mentions the Everglades again,' I said to Amanda as we headed for the train station, 'remember that they're *supposed* to be wet, OK?'

'You've already told me that ten times!' Amanda said. 'The Everglades is this big yucky swamp full of crocodiles.'

'Alligators!' I yelled.

'Alligators-shmalligators,' Amanda said with a dismissive toss of her hair. She grinned. 'He'll be so stunned by how I look that he wouldn't notice if I said it was full of polar bears.'

I've got to admit, Amanda did look pretty good. If Craig was the kind of guy who just, goes on looks, then we were home and dry. Her hair was shining and curling in all the right ways. She'd spent half the morning in front of the mirror, practising her smiling. She really does do that, you know.

'Smiles are very important,' she'd told me.

'You've got to get 'em just right. Plenty of *teeth* but no *gum*. See?' Smile! Zing! 'Dazzle 'em!'

Yeah, right. That piece of information is a whole lot of use to me while I've got these braces! I'd dazzle them, OK. I'd dazzle them with all this metalwork!

'Did you read any of Craig's letters?' I asked.

'Of course I did,' Amanda said dismissively.

'*All* of them?' I asked.

'No, not all of them,' Amanda said.

'Most of them?'

'Uh, no. Not quite,' Amanda said.

'Half of them?' I asked with a sinking feeling.

'No, not that many,' Amanda said, inspecting the reflection of her teeth in a store window.

'Two?' I asked.

Amanda made a downward gesture with her hand.

'Only *one*!' I said.

Amanda smiled at me. 'Not a *whole* one,' she said. 'His writing was kind of difficult to read. But I read about half a page. Don't worry, Stacy, I'll play it by ear. Everything will be *fine*!'

Oh, yeah, I forgot to tell you our plan. I mean, we weren't going to meet Craig *together*.

121

The idea was that I'd go into Casey's and find myself a booth. The booths in Casey's are divided off by these wooden lattice screens and the pattern of the lattice leaves plenty of holes.

Now, I was going to sit in a booth and order a shake or something, and when Amanda came in with Craig, she was going to make sure they sat in the booth next to mine.

You see, I was still really jittery about Craig saying something Amanda couldn't answer, but which Craig would *know*, that I should know about. (Amanda didn't think this was going to happen.) I explained to Amanda that if it *did* happen, I'd signal her, and she could say she needed to visit the bathroom. And I'd go in there with her, and then I could tell her what to say next.

I thought this was a pretty neat idea. Amanda said it was totally dumb. 'He'll think there's something wrong with me if I have to keep going to the bathroom every five minutes,' she'd said. 'Look, you sit in your little booth with your little milkshake, and leave all the high-class socializing to me.' And she'd patted me on the cheek. 'I know what I'm doing.'

We got to the station at twenty to one.

'OK,' Amanda said, preening her hair yet

again, 'I'll head for the platform now. You go set yourself up in Casey's.'

I grabbed her arm. 'Don't say anything dumb, Amanda,' I pleaded. 'Please don't tell him that Indian elephants have bigger ears than African elephants.'

'Look, Stacy,' Amanda said. 'I think I'm going to come up with more interesting things to talk about than the size of elephants' ears!' She gave me a shove towards Casey's.

'The Everglades have alligators,' I shouted as Amanda walked towards the platform. 'And Indian elephants have small ears!'

Oh, well. That was it. There was nothing else I could do, now. Except maybe *pray*!

I headed across the road to Casey's. It was pretty busy, but it's a big place so there were plenty of seats left. But I had to try and find two empty booths next to each other. That wasn't so easy. Casey's is circular, by the way. The kitchen and serving bars are like the hub of a big wheel, and the booths go all round the outside with big windows so you can see out.

I had hoped I'd be able to find a seat facing the station, but the only place where there were two empty booths together was clear around the far side, facing some office buildings.

The waitress appeared and I ordered a chocolate shake and a blueberry muffin. My main worry right then was that someone would come and sit in the next booth before Amanda and Craig got here.

I looked at my watch. It was exactly a quarter to one. A whole troop of butterflies in big boots did a stomping cheerleading routine in my stomach. I kept peering around. I was twisted right round, looking through the lattice to see if they were coming from the other side, when the waitress arrived with my order.

'Enjoy your food,' she said with a big professional smile. Gleam!

Enjoy? It would be a miracle if I could eat one bite. But then again, I thought, maybe I should eat something. It might calm my rocky stomach. I took a massive bite just as Amanda and Craig came walking around the curved aisle.

I sucked in my breath. A piece of muffin went the wrong way and I had a choking fit which coincided perfectly with Amanda and Craig walking past me and Amanda saying: 'This one's empty. We can sit here.'

Amanda gave me a funny look as I sat coughing and choking on my muffin.

The crumb finally cleared itself and I was able to sit back with a gasp of relief.

I wiped my eyes and glanced through the lattice screen. Craig was sitting with his back to me, so all I could see of him was the back of his head. Amanda had sat herself opposite him and I could see her perfectly clearly as she picked up the menu.

'I guess you'll be hungry after that journey,' she said. 'I know I am, and I've only walked from home.' All this was said with a big flashing smile.

'I thought you said you lived a long way from the station,' Craig said.

'Oh, yeah, I do,' Amanda said quickly. 'I didn't mean I walked all the way. My dad dropped me off. We live a few miles away.'

'I didn't think Four Corners was that big,' Craig said.

'Oh, you'd be surprised,' Amanda said. 'It's kind of *spread* recently. We live all the way out over there.' She made a long-distance gesture with her arm.

The waitress came up and they both ordered burgers and fries and Coke.

'Oh, hey,' Craig said. 'I brought this to show you.' I'd been too busy choking to death earlier to notice that he was carrying a bag with him. 'I knew you'd be interested.'

I sat up so I could see what was going on.

Craig handed some kind of notebook over to Amanda.

She looked at the cover. 'Mmm,' she said, '*The Kalahari Desert and its Wildlife.*'

'It's a new project we're working on at school,' Craig told her. 'It's not finished yet, but I thought you'd be interested.'

'Oh, I *am*,' Amanda said, opening the book. 'Wow, chapter titles,' she said. 'You've got really neat handwriting, Craig. My teacher says my writing is like a spider with ink on its feet.'

'Get out of here,' Craig laughed. 'Your writing is a lot neater than mine.'

I tried to signal Amanda but she ignored me. Amanda's writing is *just* like she said, but mine isn't – and it was *my* letters that Craig had seen. My letters with my writing.

'Hey, drawings, too,' Amanda said as she flipped through Craig's note book. 'Some of these are pretty good,' she said.

'Thanks,' Craig said.

'I'm pretty good at art,' Amanda said.

'You are?' Craig said.

I signalled frantically at Amanda behind Craig's head.

'Sure,' Amanda said, ignoring me as I waved my arms in the air.

'But I thought you said you were really

terrible at art,' Craig said, sounding a little puzzled. 'I thought it was your little sister, Amanda, who was good at art.'

There was a moment's silence as Amanda took this in.

I stopped signalling and slid down in my seat until only my eyes were showing over the back.

Amanda fixed a big grin on her face. 'Yeah,' she said, 'that's right. Amanda's *really* good at art.' She gave a hard little laugh. 'I'm no good at art at all, to be honest,' she said through teeth gritted in a smile.

Craig laughed. 'I feel really sorry for you,' he said. 'Some of the things you wrote about Amanda! She must be such a total pain!' He laughed again.

Oops. Maybe telling Craig stories about my dumb little sister, Amanda, hadn't been such a good idea after all.

Amanda glared at me for a split second through the screen. Zap! A real laser-beam glare!

She fixed her smile back in place.

'Which story about Amanda did you like best?' she asked.

'The one where she wanted you to do some homework for her and you made her slave for you for an entire week,' Craig said. 'I thought that was great!'

'Yeah,' Amanda said with a fixed grin. 'That was a *scream*, wasn't it. But did I tell you the time I found out she'd been telling people stories about me and I *beat her to a pulp*?'

Heck! I think Amanda was trying to *tell* me something. Like, I didn't have long to live.

There was a rattle of fingernails on the window of their booth. I followed the line of their eyes.

Standing outside and grinning like a demented gibbon was Rachel Goldstein. She waved and made hand signals to indicate she was coming in.

I put my hands over my face and curled up in a little ball in the corner of the bench.

# Chapter Fourteen

'Hi, Stacy!' Rachel said as she came walking along the aisle and saw me hiding in my booth. 'Hi, Amanda!'

'Hi,' Amanda said. 'What a surprise seeing you in here.'

Rachel came to a halt at their table, her dumb gibbon face grinning away as if she was waiting for someone to stuff a banana in her mouth.

'Why are you two sitting in different booths?' she asked. 'Are you fighting again?'

'Craig,' Amanda said quickly, 'this is Rachel. Rachel, this is Craig. He's visiting from Pennsylvania.'

'Hi, Craig,' Rachel said. 'So?' She looked at Amanda. 'What's with Stacy?' She looked over at me. 'Hey, why are you hiding under the table, Stacy?'

'I've brought Craig in here for a burger,' Amanda said loudly. 'Craig is my pen pal from Pennsylvania.'

'*Your* pen pal?' Rachel said. 'I thought he was Stacy's pen pal.'

Amanda let out a yell of laughter. 'Oh, Rachel,' she said, 'you're such a kidder!' She looked at Craig. 'It's a private joke,' she said to him. 'You see . . . uh . . . Rachel has only lived around here for a little while, and, uh, she always used to get my name mixed up with my sister's name.' She fixed Rachel with a deadly look. 'And sometimes she still pretends she can't remember that *I'm* Stacy.'

For a second Rachel just stood there as if her brain had overloaded and shut down.

Meanwhile, Craig had turned around in his seat and was looking at me through the holes in the screen.

'Uh, hi!' I said weakly.

Amanda stood up and stared at me over Craig's head.

'Amanda!' she said. 'What are you doing here, you pipsqueak!'

'Hi, Stacy,' I said, 'I . . . uh . . . I didn't see you there. I just came in for a . . . uh . . . a shake and a muffin . . .'

'You're both crazy!' Rachel finally managed to say. 'What the heck is going on here?'

'I came here with Craig,' Amanda said, 'and my pest of a kid sister, Amanda, *followed* me!'

She glared at me. 'I told you to stay home, Amanda!'

'It was a coincidence,' I said. 'I didn't know you were going to be here.'

'I was going to join you,' Rachel said blankly, 'but I don't think I'll bother.' She turned and wandered away, shaking her head in confusion. 'See you at school Monday, Amanda,' she called back.

'Sure thing,' I said.

Rachel paused in mid-step, looked back, shook her head again and disappeared around the curve of the aisle.

'*You're* Amanda?' Craig said, looking at me through the screen.

'That's right,' I said with a weak kind of grin. 'Hi, how are you?'

'Fine, I guess,' Craig said, looking at Amanda as if to ask what was going on.

'You came here to spy on us, didn't you, you little brat!' Amanda said to me.

'I did not,' I said. 'I can't help being in the same place at the same time. It's a free country!'

'Do you want to join us?' Craig said to me.

'No, she doesn't,' Amanda said. 'She's going straight home!'

'Thanks, I will,' I said, smiling at Craig and ignoring Amanda. I shoved in beside Amanda and looked around at them both. I was finally face to face with Craig. Those butterflies felt like they were churning around in my stomach in *tanks*! And my mouth had gone really dry.

'So?' I croaked. 'What were you talking about?'

'I can't remember,' Craig said.

'Hey,' I said, picking up Craig's project. 'Did you do all this?'

'Yes,' Craig said, leaning over the table and lifting it out of my hands. 'I don't really want it messed up.' He handed it to Amanda. 'It's taken weeks to put together. Stacy was reading it.'

'That's right,' Amanda said. She smiled at me. 'It's about the Kalgari Desert, Amanda. *You* wouldn't be interested in it at all.'

'The *Kalahari* Desert,' I corrected her.

'That's what I said,' Amanda said. She opened the book to a page on the birds that live in the desert. 'Mmm, really interesting!' she said. I suppose she sounded convincing to Craig, but I knew better.

'You can read some of it, if you want,' Craig said. 'I'd like to know what you think.'

'Maybe later,' Amanda said. 'I don't want to be rude.'

'Oh, that's OK,' Craig said. 'Go on. Have a quick read.'

'Oh, right. Fine,' Amanda said. 'I'll just read this one page then.'

It was really difficult not to keep craning around her arm to try and see what Craig had written. There were drawings of birds and a whole load of interesting-looking facts.

'So,' Craig said, smiling at me. 'You're good at art, Stacy told me?'

'Sure,' I said. 'I do a whole lot of art stuff. Drawing, painting, you know, stuff like that.'

'What kind of paint do you use?' Craig asked. 'Acrylic or gouache? Or do you use oils? My brother paints in oils, but they're really expensive.'

'I don't use oils,' I said. 'I use . . . one of the others you mentioned.'

'Gouache,' Amanda whispered from behind Craig's book. I don't know gouache from goulash. Like I've said before, I don't know *anything* about art.

'Gouache,' I said quickly. 'Uh, Stacy tells me you're really into this wildlife stuff.'

'That's right,' Craig said. 'I'm sure you'd find it interesting if you started reading up on it.'

'I guess I might,' I said.

'Maybe Stacy will lend you some of her magazines,' Craig said.

'Maybe,' I said. 'Could I take a look at your

project? When Stacy's finished reading it, of course.'

'Sure,' Craig said.

'Help yourself,' Amanda said, handing the book over to me. I could see from the glazed look in her eyes that even half a minute of reading it had been too much for her.

'What do you think?' Craig asked her.

'It's great,' Amanda said, nodding slowly. 'It's a shame I don't have the time to read the whole thing.'

'I'll send you a copy when it's finished,' Craig said. 'My Dad can get it copied where he works.'

'Terrific,' Amanda said. 'Hey, but let's not spend all *day* talking about the Killy-gargle Desert, huh?' She leaned over the table. 'What kind of sports do you like, Craig?'

Uh-oh. Craig didn't like sports at all. Stacy would know that. I gave Amanda a kick under the table. Successfully, this time!

'My older brother Brad is the sporty one,' Craig said. 'I wrote and told you how he used to make fun of me because I didn't like sports.' He sounded a little confused. (Are you *surprised*?)

'I knew that!' Amanda said, reaching down to rub her ankle. 'I was just kidding.'

'Oh, I get it,' Craig smiled. 'Like your joke

about the water in the Everglades? I'm sorry, I should be getting used to your sense of humour by now.'

The waitress arrived with their orders and Craig and Stacy started eating. What am I *saying*? I was getting as confused as Rachel. Craig and *Amanda* started eating.

*Repeat after me: I am Stacy. She is Amanda.*

I still had my nose stuck in Craig's project. Some of the stuff Craig had written in there was really amazing.

'Listen to this,' I said to Amanda, ' "The mouth brooder fish keeps its eggs in its mouth until they hatch. And even after they've hatched, the young will still go back into the parent's mouth to escape predators." '

'Wow,' Amanda said. 'That's just so totally fascinating, Sta-' *Kick*! 'Ow! that was my ankle!'

'Sorry, Stacy,' I said. 'Did I hurt you?'

'I'm sure it was just an accident,' Amanda snarled. 'You can't help being clumsy, Amanda.'

'I didn't think you'd be interested in that kind of thing,' Craig said to me.

Rats! I was supposed to be acting like the dumb little sister, Amanda, that I'd told Craig about in my letters. I'd kind of let my enthusiasm run away with me.

135

'I don't mind it in small amounts,' I said. 'I guess I just have a short attention span. My teachers are always telling me I don't concentrate enough. Stacy, here, is the real brain of the family. Isn't that right, Stacy?'

'We can't all be brilliant,' Amanda said.

'That's right,' I said, shaking my head sadly. 'Mom is always saying, "Amanda, if only you put as much effort into your schoolwork as Stacy does, you'd do much better." ' I looked at Amanda. 'Isn't that what Mom always says, Stacy?'

'Yes,' Amanda said stonily. 'I guess it is.' (It is, too! It's *exactly* what Mom says!)

I sighed. 'I guess I'm just a little *slow*, and that's all there is to it.'

'But you're totally brilliant at art,' Amanda said. 'And you're really good at sports. I think that's just as important as the kind of stuff *I'm* good at. Like, I really wish I was as popular at school as you are, Amanda.' She looked at Craig. 'You wouldn't believe how popular Amanda is. Absolutely everyone likes her. And she's head cheerleader, aren't you, Amanda? And not everyone could do a really difficult job like that.' She gave me a couple of over-friendly pats on the back. 'You really should stop being so *modest* about yourself, Amanda. I just wish I was more like you!'

'No,' I said. 'I'm dumb! Dumb! Dumb! Dumb! I mean, any idiot can be a cheerleader. It takes a really brainy person to do stuff like that project on whales you did a couple of months ago.' I looked at Craig. 'Did Stacy tell you about that? It was totally brilliant. I was *so* jealous.'

'If you remember,' Amanda said. 'it was *you* who showed me how to do the drawings.' She smiled at Craig. 'My drawings of the whales were completely useless until Amanda showed me how to do them.'

Craig looked a little dumbfounded. Of course, *he* didn't know what the heck was going on. As far as he could make out, each of us was praising the other to the skies and putting ourselves down like crazy.

'I remember you telling me about the whale project,' Craig said, looking at Amanda. 'That was one of the first things you wrote to me about.'

'It was?' Amanda said. 'Oh! Yeah, it *was*! Uh, would you excuse me for a minute, Craig. I need to go to the bathroom.' She shoved me off the seat. 'And Amanda wants to go to the bathroom, too,' she said, grabbing hold of my wrist.

'I do not,' I said.

'Oh, yes you do,' Amanda said. 'I can tell by the way you were wriggling.'

'I was not wriggling!'

'You were. Come on, Amanda. We'll be back in a minute, Craig.'

Amanda dragged me to the ladies room.

'What was all that about?' I asked once we were behind the door.

'What were all those cracks about Amanda being so dumb?' Amanda demanded. 'Do you think I don't know what you were up to back there?'

'What's the big problem?' I asked. 'He thinks *you're* Stacy. He thinks *I'm* the dumb one.'

'Just cut out the anti-Amanda stuff, right?' Amanda said. 'Because if you don't, I'm going to tell Craig exactly what *is* going on here.'

'You wouldn't,' I said.

'Just try me, Stacy,' Amanda said. 'And then who's going to look *really* dumb?'

'OK,' I said, feeling a little panicky. 'I won't say anything else about how dumb I am if you don't say anything about how dumb – ' I stopped. I was getting very confused.

'Just cut out the dumb Amanda jokes,' Amanda said. 'And no more funny stories about me in your letters, either. OK?'

'OK,' I agreed.

We went back out and sat down.

'Is everything OK?' Craig asked.

'Sure,' I said. Amanda gave me a kick.

'Everything is just fine,' she said with a big smile.

'Great,' Craig said. 'I've been thinking, wouldn't it be fun for the two of us to do a project together sometime?'

'Yeah,' Amanda said. 'Why not? Did you have something in mind?'

'I've got a few ideas,' Craig said. 'But I'd like to know what you'd be interested in working on.'

'What I'd be interested in working on?' Amanda said. 'Oh. Right. You want me to come up with some ideas.'

'Yeah,' Craig said. 'What are you *really* interested in?'

Amanda was silent for a few moments. I sneaked a look at her. Oh, no! She had that blank look on her face that meant she'd just gone brain-dead.

I decided I'd better help her out.

'Didn't you tell me you were really interested in – '

'Black holes!' Amanda blurted, interrupting me.

'Sorry?' Craig said.

Amanda blinked at him. 'Black holes,' she

repeated. 'They're collapsed Super Giant stars.'

Craig grinned. 'I know they are,' he said. 'I didn't think you knew anything about astronomy.'

'Neither did I,' Amanda breathed.

Wow! So Pippa's sublemonade learning really did work! (I made a mental note to sneak into Amanda's room some other night soon and whisper, 'Give all your money to Stacy' in her ear.)

'We could do a project on astronomy, if you'd really like to,' Craig said.

'Hot stars are blue,' Amanda murmured. 'Less hot stars are red.' She looked at me. 'How the heck do I know that?'

'Hi, guys,' said a totally unexpected voice. 'Mind if I join you?'

I stared at Dad with my mouth open.

He was just standing there by our booth as though he'd popped out of nowhere like a genie.

What was he doing here?

'Huggg guggg . . .' I managed to say as he blasted one of his huge cheerful smiles around the booth and took a seat next to Craig.

'So,' he said, 'what are you guys up to?'

# Chapter Fifteen

'Uh, Craig,' Amanda said, 'this is my dad.'

'Hello, Mr Allen,' Craig said. 'Pleased to meet you.'

My dad flashed another smile. 'It's nice to meet you, Craig,' he said. 'Stacy's told us a lot about you.'

I gave a nervous little laugh. 'What brings you over this way, Dad?' I asked.

Keep cool. Keep calm. There was a hundred to one chance that we might *still* get away with this.

'Oh, I was just passing by in the car,' Dad said. 'And I thought to myself, hey, I'm right near the place where Stacy and Amanda are meeting up with Stacy's friend Craig. So, I thought to myself, why not stop off and say hi?'

'You were just passing by?' Amanda said.

'That's about the size of it,' Dad said. 'Can I hijack one of your fries, Amanda?' He reached across the table and picked a few fries off Amanda's plate.

'Sure,' I said quickly. 'Help yourself.'

I gave Craig a quick glance to see if he'd spotted that Dad called Amanda Amanda. And that was the first time I noticed that he had a little smile on his face. A very *strange* little smile.

'Passing by where?' Amanda asked Dad.

'Excuse me?' Dad said, chewing fries.

'You said you were passing by,' Amanda said. 'So where were you going?'

Dad smiled. 'Past,' he said. 'Like I told you.' He turned to Craig. 'Is this your first visit to these parts?' he asked.

'I've been to Indianapolis a few times,' Craig said. 'We have relatives living there. But I've never been up here before.'

'And what do you think of your visit so far?' Dad asked him. 'Have my girls been keeping you entertained?'

Craig nodded slowly. 'Yes,' he said. 'It's been very interesting.' He smiled that smile again.

Dad looked across at us. 'So what do you three have planned for the rest of the day?' he asked.

'Nothing in particular,' Amanda said. 'We just thought we'd hang out and stuff.'

'Hey,' Dad said, 'I just had an idea. Why don't I drive you back to our house? I'm sure your mom would like to meet Craig. Then I could drive you back here in time for Craig's train back to Indianapolis.' He looked at Craig. 'What do you say, Craig?'

'Great,' Craig said. 'I'd really like that.'

So *that* was it! I'd been sitting there wondering where Dad could have been going that would take him past the train station. Then it suddenly clicked. He hadn't been driving *past* at all. He'd come here to find us and take us back home. And I knew *why*, too. Mom had set it up. Mom wanted to meet Craig.

I should have *known* Mom would come up with some sneaky way of wrecking our plans to keep Craig away from the house.

'Fine, let's do that,' Dad said. 'You guys finish your lunch. I'll go pay the bill and then we can head home.'

He got up and made his way over to the cashier.

I was finished! Doomed! There was no way in the world that Amanda and I were going to be able to keep up pretending to be each other once we'd gotten back home.

'That was nice of your dad,' Craig said.

'Yeah,' Amanda said. 'Our parents are nice, aren't they, Amanda?' She leaned across the

143

table towards Craig. 'But they're kind of weird, too.'

'Weird?' Craig said. 'In what way weird?'

'They've got this, uh, kind of *game* they play at home,' Amanda said. 'They like to call us by the wrong names. Like, sometimes they'll spend the entire day calling me Amanda and calling her – ' she hooked a thumb in my direction, ' – Stacy. So don't be surprised if something like that happens when we get back to our place.' She looked around at me. 'Isn't that right, Amanda? Isn't that what they do?'

I opened my mouth to speak. Then I saw that *smile* on Craig's face again.

'It's no good,' I said miserably. 'I give up!'

'What do you mean?' Amanda asked me.

'Forget it!' I said. 'I've got to confess.'

'Confess what, Stacy?' Craig asked me.

I looked at him. 'I'm really sorry about this,' I said. 'I don't know how to . . . What did you call me?'

'Stacy,' Craig said with a laugh. He pointed at me. 'You're Stacy.' He pointed at Amanda. 'And you're Amanda.' He laughed again. 'Do I get a prize for guessing?'

'You knew!' Amanda said. 'You knew the whole time? How did you know?'

'I didn't know the whole time,' Craig said. 'I didn't figure it out for a while. But I'd have had to have been pretty dumb not to notice what was going on. I mean, let's be honest, you're not the world's best actors.' He grinned at Amanda. 'The Killy-gargle Desert?'

'I guess we did make kind of a *mess* of it,' Amanda said. 'I nearly *died* when Rachel walked in.'

'Yeah, that was funny,' Craig said.

'Look, Craig,' Amanda said, putting her arm around me. 'It might look like Stacy here is a total nut, but she isn't really. The truth is that she sent you that picture of me because she thought you might not want to be her pen pal any more if you knew she was only ten. And then, when you were coming to visit, the whole thing kind of – '

'Escalated,' I said. I looked at Craig. 'You must think I'm really dumb.'

'Yes,' Craig said. 'I do think you're dumb.' He smiled at me. 'I think you're dumb for thinking I wouldn't want to write to you because you were ten. I mean, what's the big deal? I really like getting your letters. I want us to keep writing to each other.' He grinned. 'Unless you think I'm too *old* to be your pen pal.'

'You don't think I'm crazy?' I said hopefully. 'You don't think I'm the weirdest person you've ever met?'

Craig laughed. 'I think you're both pretty crazy,' he said. 'But, hey, I *like* crazy people.'

'Could you do me one big favour?' I asked.

'Sure,' Craig said. 'What?'

'Don't let my mom and dad know what's been going on.'

'My lips are sealed!' Craig said. 'On one condition.'

'What?' I asked.

'That you send me a photo of *you* with your next letter,' Craig said. 'And that we work on a project together.'

I smiled my first totally happy smile for days. 'You bet!' I said.

Dad came back over to our table.

'OK, kids?' he said. 'Everyone set?'

'Yup,' I said. 'Let's go home, Dad. I'd really like Mom to meet Craig.'

* * *

Amanda and I were sitting on the low wall in front of our house that night. It was pretty late and the clear, dark sky was full of stars. For the first time in *days* I was feeling totally relaxed.

The afternoon had gone really well. Craig and my mom had hit it off right away and we'd all had a really good time together until we had to take Craig back to the station for his train to Indianapolis.

Mom had even invited Craig to stay with us another time. And Craig said he'd really like that, so it looked like he'd be visiting again. And on the next visit we'd have time to go to the wildlife park.

'So what's *that* one called?' Amanda asked, pointing up at a bright twinkle right in the middle of the sky.

I consulted my beginners' book.

'Turnip,' I said. 'Otherwise known as the Vegetable Star.'

'Boy, who'd give a star a name like that?' Amanda said.

'I just did,' I said.

Amanda looked at me. 'Harty-har-har,' she said. 'I'm trying to show an interest in this astrology stuff, Stacy. Quit fooling around. What's it really called?'

'I think it's Polaris,' I said, thumbing through the book and trying to read it in the dark. I found the star chart.

'Yeah,' I said. 'It's Polaris, OK. Otherwise known as the North Star.' I held the book up against the sky. 'See?'

'Not really,' Amanda said. 'Hold it over here. What am I supposed to be looking for?'

I leaned back, trying to line the map in the book up with the real sky. 'You see that constellation that looks kind of like a saucepan?' I said.

'No, I – *oops!*' As Amanda leaned back to try and see better, she gave a yelp and fell backwards off the wall, grabbing me as she went.

'Amand – *ow!*' I yelled as I found myself on my back on the front lawn with Amanda lying beside me and giggling.

'*Now* I can see it,' Amanda said. 'What's the constellation called?'

'It's called the Big Bear,' I told her. I pointed up. 'And somewhere around there is the Little Bear.'

'Ahh!' Amanda said. 'A big bear and a little bear. Just like us.'

I couldn't help laughing.

'Hey, Amanda,' I said. 'Thanks for what you said to Craig at Casey's. It really helped.'

'It was nothing,' Amanda said. 'What are big sisters for?'

Now *there's* a good question!

'You know something?' I said. 'You're not *always* a total bimbo.'

'Well, it's nice of you to say so,' Amanda said with a grin. 'And you're not always a total nerd. Just most of the time.'

We both started laughing.

We were still laughing when Mom came out to see what we were doing.

She looked down at us as we lay there side by side in the grass.

'Do I have crazy kids, or what?' she said.

I smiled up at her.

'You don't know even half of it,' I said.

And with any luck that was just the way it was going to stay!

Look out for sisters Stacy and Amanda in **Little Sister Book** 7, coming soon in 1996 from Red Fox!

*Other great reads* ✒ *from* **Red Fox**

Further Red Fox titles that you might enjoy reading are listed on the following pages. They are available in bookshops or they can be ordered directly from us.

If you would like to order books, please send this form and the money due to:

ARROW BOOKS, BOOKSERVICE BY POST, PO BOX 29, DOUGLAS, ISLE OF MAN, BRITISH ISLES. Please enclose a cheque or postal order made out to Arrow Books Ltd for the amount due, plus 75p per book for postage and packing to a maximum of £7.50, both for orders within the UK. For customers outside the UK, please allow £1.00 per book.

NAME_____

ADDRESS_____

_____

*Please print clearly.*

Whilst every effort is made to keep prices low, it is sometimes necessary to increase cover prices at short notice. If you are ordering books by post, to save delay it is advisable to phone to confirm the correct price. The number to ring is THE SALES DEPARTMENT 071 (if outside London) 973 9700.

*Other great reads from Red Fox*

## Little Sister Series by Allan Frewin Jones

### LITTLE SISTER 1 – THE GREAT SISTER WAR

Meet Stacy Allen, a ten year old tomboy and a bit of a bookworm. Now meet her blue-eyed blonde sister, Amanda, just turned 13 and a fully-fledged teenager. Stacy thinks Amanda's a total airhead and Amanda calls Stacy and her gang the nerds; they have the biggest love-hate relationship of the century and that can only mean one thing – war.
ISBN 0 09 938381 0   £2.99

### LITTLE SISTER 2 – MY SISTER, MY SLAVE

When Amanda starts to become a school slacker, Mom is ready to take drastic action – pull Amanda out of the cheerleading squad! So the sisters make a deal; Stacy will help Amanda with her school work in return for two whole days of slavery. But Amanda doesn't realize that when her little sister's boss, two days means 48 *whole* hours of chores – snea-kee!
ISBN 0 09 938391 8   £2.99

### LITTLE SISTER 3 – STACY THE MATCHMAKER

Amanda is mad that the school Barbie doll, Judy McWilliams, has got herself a boyfriend, and to make things worse it's hunky Greg Masterson, the guy Amanda has fancied for ages. Stacy feels that it's her duty as sister to fix Amanda's lovelife and decides to play cupid and do a bit of matchmaking, with disastrous results!
ISBN 0 09 938401 9   £2.99

### LITTLE SISTER 4 – COPYCAT

Cousin Laine is so coo-ool! She's a glamorous 18 year old and wears gorgeous clothes, and has got a boyfriend with a car. When Stacy and Amanda's parents go away for a week leaving Laine in charge, 13 year old Amanda decides she wants to be just like her cousin and begins to copy Laine's every move . . .
ISBN 0 09 938411 6   £2.99

*Other great reads* from Red Fox

## Little Sister Series by Allan Frewin Jones

LITTLE SISTER 5 – SNEAKING OUT

Pop star Eddie Eden is *the* guy every cool teenager is
swooning over and Amanda has got a mega crush on him.
Amanda is in love big time and when Eddie's tour dates are
announced she's desperate to see her idol – but Mom and
Dad don't want her out so late. So what else is there for a
love-struck girl to do but sneak out?
ISBN 0 09 938421 3   £2.99

LITTLE SISTER 6 – SISTER SWITCH

Stacy's pen pal, Craig, loves her letters and all his friends are
jealous when they see her photo – so he fixes a date. This is
bad news for the Allen sisters. Stacy hates her mousy hair
and freckles so much that she sent him a photo of pretty
Amanda. But if Stacy can persuade Amanda to swop places
and be *her* for one day she might be able to keep her secret
identity safe . . .
ISBN 0 09 938431 0   £2.99

# Join the RED FOX Reader's Club

The Red Fox Reader's Club is for readers of all ages. All you have to do is ask your local bookseller or librarian for a Red Fox Reader's Club card. As an official Red Fox Reader you only have to borrow or buy eight Red Fox books in order to qualify for your own Red Fox Reader's Clubpack – full of exciting surprises! If you have any difficulty obtaining a Red Fox Reader's Club card please write to: Random House Children's Books Marketing Department, 20 Vauxhall Bridge Road, London SW1V 2SA.